THE SPACE SHE MADE FOR ME

A Collection of Sapphic Short Stories

Jo Boyle

ISBN: 978-0-6452773-3-3

The prompts that inspired these stories can be found at:
https://blog.reedsy.com/creative-writing-prompts/

Cover design by: Mariana Carrino

For all of the brave women who brought us to where we are;
And for those who keep fighting a war that is not yet won.

They found her dead;
Lying in a field of Tulips.
But she wasn't famous,
Nor was she pretty.
she wasn't a mother;
Nor someone's lover.
her work was honest,
But inglorious.
So the media decided she had not died at all,
And the Tulips were left to flourish.

1

*Write about someone stuck in an endless cycle
who finally manages to break free.*

AMY'S BLISS

One

B liss Collins was a mistake.
No less so than Katie Bramich, it turned out.

As Bliss traversed the gloomy, muddy trail, enshrouded by a thick forest of giant Man Ferns and scented by broken, moss devoured Blackwood, she imagined the vista from the peak. It would be magnificent. The viewing platform jutted out over a rocky face, and far below, a cascading fall that bled into a river rabid with water that frothed and foamed around its snaking, tree-lined bends.

The morning was cool and cloudy, and Bliss's breaths slipped out of her in white puffs, like exploded pearls. As one foot fell in front of the other along the steep incline, her calf muscles burned. But she didn't mind that. It was an honest exchange between mind and body, a communication that couldn't be forged.

Not like that of the chatter between humans. Humans who threw around words like 'friendship' and 'forever', until they became words like 'I don't understand you' and 'Let's just call it a day.'

Talk was overrated anyway. No one really said what they meant, and barely a soul meant what they said. Everyone was just a bundle of lies rolled up in a ball of insecurity, slicked in sticky pretence and sugar-coated with hollow grins. None of that alleviated her loneliness. It only exacerbated it to... well, to *this*: a final trek up a lonely mountain.

Bliss had never been able to play the game, although she'd tried for an inordinate number of years. She had been abandoned by her mother, belittled by her father, and found temporary solace in fleeting friendships with people who never really understood her on a layer beyond the superficial. Finally, after realising she was unworthy of anything more meaningful, she decided she was probably never meant to exist in the first place.

But that was something she could fix. All of this other... *stuff*, she simply had no control over. She didn't want what other people wanted, and she didn't know how to pretend that she did. She couldn't blend into the fold, always seemed to be sticking out of it like some raging, catastrophic tumour. She'd heard people talking about tribes, but no tribe ever came for her that she imagined as hers. Belonging was surely fine when you knew how. But what if you didn't? What if people could be accidents; lived entire lives never having found their place? If Bliss was a mistake, she was also the fix. If she was the problem, she was also the solution.

Maybe it would hurt.

But it wouldn't hurt for long.

Then all of this failure would be done.

As the dense canopy of treetops opened to a great grey sky, the metal platform appeared.

Two

But it wasn't empty. A woman was there, pressed to the railing with her back to Bliss, staring out over the canyon. She carried no camera, as many visitors to the picturesque region often did. She only carried herself, in pewter puffer jacket and blue jeans. Her hair was black as crow's feathers, long and taken by a cold breeze that swept Bliss's own blonde locks across her eyes. The woman gripped the railing with white-knuckled intensity, and then lifted her head to the forbidding sky.

Bliss looked through yellow wisps over her own shoulder, down the trail and into the dark forest behind. No one had followed. It was just the two of them. All Bliss had to do was wait for the woman to leave. She turned to the loner, who evidently had no intention of waiting, because in that moment she hopped and lifted her right leg over the railing.

Bliss hollered, "No! Wait!"

The woman's head jerked, the bar between her legs at her crotch; her hands gripping tight; her face at once pale and shadowed with grief. She stared at Bliss with her wide, suddenly familiar eyes, then threw her left leg over the railing. She lowered herself so that only her toes touched the edge of the platform, and then leaned back and peered down.

Bliss rushed three steps forward, and then halted for fright that the woman would let go. She raised her palms and begged, "Please, don't do this. You don't have to do this."

The woman's features were not twisted with torment, but rather resigned to some harsh reality. A tear bled from her eye, and she whispered, "I'm sorry."

"No," Bliss breathed. "I'm the one who's sorry."

Green eyes narrowed. "Why should you be sorry?"

"Because if you do this, I'm following you right into this ravine."

"Don't be stupid."

"I mean it."

"If you throw yourself over this ledge, that's nothing to do with me."

"Isn't it?"

"I don't even know you."

For the first time, Bliss cared enough to regret her bobbed, bleached hair. "My name is Bliss Collins. I live in Ambleside. I... I'm really shitty at keeping indoor plants alive."

The shadow in that gaze seemed to dispel, if only for a moment. "Killing indoor plants is no reason to throw yourself over this railing, Bliss Collins."

Bliss shuffled closer, under a watchful eye. She looked out over the expansive canyon, backdrop to this woman who needed for her to say something that might invalidate her intentions; intentions that only moments before had been Bliss's own.

"You think what you do doesn't matter. It does, and it's never mattered more than it does right now. If you let go, and I don't follow you, I will be forever haunted by your face. As pleasing as it is, I don't want that, and I don't think you do either."

"You think I'm selfish. Just like everyone else. I'm doing them a favour. Why do you think I'm hanging off this shitting railing? They don't want me, Bliss. I'm faulty. A mistake."

A mistake. How tragic it sounded coming from someone else.

Bliss said, "Not to me."

"You don't even know me."

"I do, actually. You're Amy Briggs."

Amy's brow wrinkled. "You only know that because my father is Robert Briggs, in the paper every week with his infernal preaching."

"That's not how I know you."

"Look, Bliss Collins, this has nothing to do with you. I am not responsible for you or what you decide to do with your life."

Bliss stepped closer. Amy tensed like a boxer expecting a kidney punch. Bliss offered gently, "I know you, because we attended the same high school. I was a grade below you." Amy's stare was searching. Bliss said, "Maybe you don't remember because I wasn't popular. I spent most of my time hiding in the library to avoid the... the teasing."

Amy muttered as if she were apologising for an entire grade, "There's lots of *stupid* in high school. Anyway, it was a long time ago."

"It was. And I'd forgotten something important about it until this very moment."

"What's that?"

"You."

Amy's gaping surprise was coupled with a one-word whisper, "Me?"

Bliss explained, "We had both arrived late at the school gates this one day, both dropped off by our fathers. Only, mine berated me as I got out of the car. Maybe he called me *dumb shit*, or *dim wit*. Those were his go-to's when I was growing up. I looked over at you, embarrassed that you'd heard, which I assumed you *had* judging by the look on your face." Amy's mouth opened, but nothing came out of it. Then her chin dropped to her chest. Bliss said, "Can I show you something?" Amy looked up and gave a tentative nod. Bliss reached behind and took the wallet from her back pocket. She removed from it a wrinkled bit of paper and dropped the wallet onto the deck. She unfolded the weary slip and shuffled close – to within touching distance – then held the note up to Amy's eyes. Dark pupils darted across the page, and then those green depths filled.

Bliss returned the slip to her pocket and said, "I found the note in my locker that same day. I didn't recognise the handwriting, but I knew it was you." Bliss recited from memory:

"He doesn't see you for who you are.

He sees you for who he isn't.

Enemies lie. Loved ones lie.

They all lie the same:

With jealous tongues.

Don't believe him.

You are magnificent."

Tears sluiced Amy's ghost-pale cheeks.

Bliss said, "I tried to find you the next day, but then I heard you'd been taken out of school. For medical reasons, they said." Amy's face twisted, and her cries pimpled Bliss's skin. The sound travelled like a grief-stricken wind, bounced and echoed and carried to every corner of the canyon, all the way down to the churning rapids below.

Bliss wanted to reach out, to secure the woman from falling. But she was frightened that Amy would rebel and then plummet. Instead, she murmured, "Were you lying to me, too, Amy? Because I believed you that day. You made me feel seen. For once in my life, I felt special. Were you... were you just *lying*, like everybody else?"

Amy's voice was thin with pleading. "*No.*"

"But you don't remember me."

Amy released a hand from the railing, driving a gasp into Bliss's throat. Then Amy brushed Bliss's wind-swept hair. "I do remember. You were a brunette back then, and your hair was longer. And your name wasn't Bliss Collins. It was Katie Bramich."

Bliss would've been pleased –*thrilled,* even – if not for the grim circumstance. "Please, Amy..." Bliss looked down. They were so high up that tree hoods looked like garden peas. Her voice trembled. "Please climb back over."

A faint smile touched Amy's lips. "You wrote poetry. And you cleaned the graffiti off the toilet walls; putrid taunts left by pubescent teens against *other* pubescent teens."

"How... how do you know that?"

"Because I saw you, Katie. But you didn't see me seeing you, did you? Perhaps you didn't want to. Perhaps you saw me as others did; as a mistake."

"That's not true."

"My father saw me as a mistake. To this day that's how he sees me."

"You are not a mistake, Amy Briggs. I've wanted to tell you ever since that day, you... *you* are magnificent. Please, Amy..." Bliss was sobbing. She'd been so empty for so long, but now she was awash with emotion. Something else, as well, stirred inside of her. Something akin to hope. "Please don't let it be that I find you here after all these years, only to..."

Three

"My father saw me as a mistake. To this day that's how he sees me."

"You are not a mistake, Amy Briggs. I've wanted to tell you ever since that day, you... *you* are magnificent. Please, Amy..." Katie was sobbing. Amy's heart was aching. What if everything Katie was saying was just a selfless effort to stop Amy's plunge? But the *note.* Katie had been holding onto it all these years. It was in her wallet, for goodness' sake. Amy had been so confused about her feelings back then, and when she'd finally confided in her parents, she had been outcast. Torn out of school and sent away, and never again comfortable admitting the truth. Now here was Katie Bramich, a.k.a. Bliss Collins, determined to make her face it.

Amy and Kate had only ever exchanged hello's; smiling, kind, but not ever followed up with what could be called *meaningful* conversation. Amy had been drawn to Kate in a manner 'unbecoming', and the situation leant itself to only one solution. And so Amy had kept her distance. It had worked, right up until that day; the day that Katie's father had treated his daughter with unapologetic disdain. Amy's rant to the preacher that night had prompted an inquisition, an onslaught of accusation under which Amy finally buckled. Painfully aware of the holy man's stance, she had hoped that being her father, he might come to understand things a little differently. But he would not let go his bigotry, sending Amy away and setting her on a path of self-destruction. She never imagined that Katie might have given her a second thought. After so many years of rejecting her own feelings, she doubted *anyone* would.

Time had changed them both. But damn if Amy didn't still feel something of what she felt back then. A connection she had not since known; not *let* herself know.

"Please don't let it be that I find you here after all these years, only to..."

Inexplicable. Powerful. Distracting.

Amy's foot slipped.

2

Write a story inspired by the phrase, "It's hardly brain surgery."

EVERLEE AND WALNUT

One

Sitting outside the Moh-Kah Face Café on an overcast autumn day, Taylor scolded Nat from across the table with an ostentatious eye roll. "It's hardly brain surgery," the plucky redhead asserted.

"No. I'm guessing brain surgery would be easier."

"Just *ask* her, for goodness' sake. Assuming she ever comes back."

Nat gave her head a shake. "A brain doesn't look much more than a wet cauliflower to me. How hard is it to dissect a cauliflower?"

"You know what, I get it. She *is* gorgeous. And let's face it, you're no Miss Universe." Nat pursed her lips, only mildly offended. Taylor chuckled. "Hey, I didn't say you were a giant *ugmo* or anything."

"I appreciate the pity you bestow upon me that I might enjoy our friendship."

"What can I say? I'm a humanitarian." Taylor lifted the mug to her lips, and then thumped it back down again. "Oh my god! Is that her?"

Nat followed Taylor's wide-eyed gape across the quadrant. Everlee Bertrand was dressed in a sharp black coat that hugged her curvaceous frame to the knees, and she strode with purpose in their direction, causing Nat's palms to sweat.

Taylor gripped Nat's wrist. "If you don't say something, I will."

As Everlee drew nearer, Natalie dropped her eyes and hugged the warm cup between her hands. The clacking of heels grew louder.

Taylor's annoying rasp made its garish assault. "Hello there!" The clacking halted. "It's Everlee, isn't it?" Nat raised the cup to her lips and peered over the rim. Everlee carried the look of the mildly amused, a look Nat had admired countless times from afar.

Everlee replied, "Yes. I'm sorry, have we met?"

"Not officially. I'm Taylor Greene. My daughter sits in on your reading group every Tuesday."

Everlee married a palm with her forehead. "Oh, of course. Tammy's mum. She's a very bright young lady."

"She just adores you. And she misses you. She says Miss Bertrand hasn't been reading at the library for weeks."

"I've... I've been out of town, unfortunately. An extended break. I do miss the kids." Everlee's attention drifted to Nat, and she smiled. "I've seen you at the library too, haven't I?"

Nat opened her mouth to reply when the blunderbuss exhorted, "This is my brain surgeon, Nat Parker." Nat shot the mischief-maker a scowl. Taylor patted Nat's shoulder. "Ever since the operation, she takes me places. Guilt for her overzealous scalpel, I imagine. I forget things: faces, places, underwear."

Nat blurted, "I'm in administration. I am *not* a neurosurgeon." Everlee hid a grin behind her fingers. Nat stammered, "I... I wouldn't make a good neurosurgeon. I've only just this morning compared the brain to a... well, to a garden vegetable." Thanks to Taylor's explosive chortle, Nat prayed the earth might open up and swallow her, chair and all.

Everlee asked, "Did you have a particular vegetable in mind?"

Cheeks burned. Nat replied, "A cauliflower, actually."

Everlee's right eyebrow tweaked. "*Actually*," she said, "*I* think the brain more resembles a walnut." Everlee Bertrand gave the most evocative grin Nat Parker had ever seen. "It's nice to finally meet you both," she said, then breezed past them into the café.

Nat's heart was still fluttering when Taylor thumped her shoulder and demanded, "You have to go in there."

"What? *Why?*"

"That woman is just waiting to pull a Florence Nightingale on some hapless sap."

"Oh. Well. Thanks."

"Pity is your friend. Stop overthinking it and get in there... before she disappears again."

Two

Nat's tummy was cartwheeling when she fell in line behind the slightly taller Everlee. She smoothed her eyes over the woman's lustrous chestnut mane, while her nose appreciated the sanguine scent of jasmine.

Nat was trying to divine a witty opening when Everlee looked over her shoulder and said, "Are you trying to decide if my brain resembles a cauliflower more than a walnut?"

"I would never compare your brain to anything as mundane as brassica."

Everlee chuckled. Then she turned. "Are you sure you should leave your patient alone out there?"

"She's not *too* dangerous. And she's scheduled for a lobotomy, which her family are very excited about."

"Well, don't be too hard on her."

"No?"

"She seems genuinely concerned about you." Nat turned. Taylor was stickybeaking from her seat through the open door, and she suddenly sat back and lifted her phone to her nose.

Nat met the enchanting green of Everlee's smiling eyes. "Listen, I... I don't usually... but I was wondering... would you... would you like to maybe get a drink sometime?" The inviting smile didn't vanish, exactly. But it faded, and Nat silently cursed her pushy friend.

Everlee replied, "That sounds lovely. Really. But I... I'm heading out of state in three weeks."

God, Nat. You've just made a complete fool of yourself. As if she wants to be hit on by some random-

Everlee touched Nat's arm. "That's not a brush-off, Nat Parker. I don't do frivolous. I could be gone for a while, and I don't want to start anything that might make it harder for me to leave."

Not particularly good at reading people, Nat regardless believed her. "Do you have a pen?"

Everlee reached inside her jacket and pulled from her breast a silver-barrelled jotter. Nat reached around Everlee's hip and stole a serviette from the counter. She took the pen and scribbled her name and number, and finished off with a crude sketch. Then she palmed Everlee both items. "Just in case you change your mind."

Everlee scanned the napkin, and the corner of her mouth curled upward. "A walnut?"

"Frivolous, I know."

"Maybe. But in the most adorable way."

A lady called from the counter, "Ev B." Everlee pocketed the slip, then collected her order. She returned to Nat with a guarded smile. "It was nice to meet you, Natalie. I mean that." She headed towards the exit, leaving Nat with a weight in her chest. But it wasn't the weight of rejection. It was the weight of memory. A memory of someone close to her who hadn't known how to live. A memory of a father who, even on his death bed, would not reveal his heart. A man who had branded every opportunity of affection as a type of malady that would metastasise if not suppressed.

Nat lunged off her feet and burst through the door, and Taylor declared, "She's headed towards Buckley!"

Nat nodded and blundered her way forward through the glut of bodies on the footpath. She caught glimpse and called into the crowd, "Everlee. Wait." A moment later she was face to face with Everlee's bemusement.

Catching her breath, Nat said, "Give me three weeks."

"I... I don't understand."

"You said you're leaving in three weeks. I'll take them."

Everlee retorted, "I told you, I don't do frivolous."

"That's... that's not what I'm asking."

"Then what are you asking? I don't understand what you expect."

Nat stepped close so that their toes were almost touching. The fact that Everlee allowed it gave Nat just a glimmer of hope. "Are you familiar with an author named Jamie Stevens?" The stress-lines between Everlee's eyebrows vanished. Nat recounted, "'There is a familiar dank in that dark dwelling. Scaly trunks and gnarled limbs and voiceless, heckling whispers. And no light. Night on night, no light. I endured in that bitter lodging, unwitting, until out of the mire came a flicker. A flare without feint nor form. Fevered I followed, somehow sure that if I could...'"

Everlee murmured, "'...sure that if I could stay with it, if I could just keep it close, I would be privy to some fantastic truth, the likes of which no new darkness could diminish; no old deceit could dislodge; that no further revelation could upend.'"

Everlee's affecting recitation gave the words a beauty Nat had not before appreciated. She was left speechless by it, even more so by the intensity with which Everlee now looked at her.

A ringtone from Everlee's coat broke the spell. She fished a phone from a pocket; grimaced after checking the screen. "I... I really need to go."

Not knowing what else she could say, and realising just how invasive her proximity, Nat stepped back.

Everlee latched onto her fingers. "Dinner, tonight. Franco's, seven o'clock."

Giddy with delight, Nat replied hoarsely, "I'll be there."

"Don't be late, Walnut." Everlee Bertrand's warm touch slipped away, and she departed with a grin.

Three

Nat wasn't late for dinner that night. Nor was she late for dinner the next. What began as two women enjoying a meal together, became two women enjoying a show. Then it became two women walking beaches and visiting museums. It became two women debating ideas and discussing philosophies. It became two women laughing together, contemplating together, sharing in a manner that never digressed to impatience or ill will.

When Nat wasn't with Everlee, she was thinking about her. About what wonderful place they might discover next, about what new things she might learn about a woman who was in the first instance guarded, but had since opened like a field of wildflowers; her colours rich, her mind sharp, her zest for life contagious.

As overwhelming as Nat's experience, the two had never touched beyond the holding of hands. Nat desired Everlee in every sense, there was no mistaking that. And she was almost positive Everlee felt the same way. But for whatever reason, Everlee was hesitating, and Nat wouldn't do anything to endanger a connection she felt on such a new and intimate plane. She had had the most fulfilling three weeks of her life, and she wanted Everlee to know that her friendship was not predicated on the notion that Everlee would give more than she was willing. Nat hoped more than anything that in whatever form, Everlee would want to continue the friendship moving forward.

On the last night, Nat received a text. Everlee wanted to stay in, and offered to cook for Nat at the apartment.

After a finely prepared spread of stuffed mushrooms and eggplant parma, they sat on the couch together in the glow of candlelight, and sipped on a Moscato which gave a delightful rose to Everlee's cheeks.

The contemplative lady ran a finger around the rim of her glass. "What is it you want from life, Nat Parker?" She looked up at Nat with her patience and her intelligence, and – Nat wanted to believe – her passion.

Nat took a sip of the pale yellow nectar, cool and sweet on her tongue. "Up until three weeks ago, I had no clue. I *thought* I did, but..." Everlee's unflinching eye burned into her, so intently that fire rushed Nat's skin. Nat added with a murmur, "What I want from life, Ev, is to not waste a *single* moment of it."

Out of those kind eyes a tear fell. Everlee uncrossed her legs and placed the glass on the coffee table, so gently that it barely made a sound. She sat on the edge of the seat, with her elbows on her knees and her fingers at her mouth. The room was so quiet and Nat so still, that she could hear – could sense – every movement, every impact on the air that Everlee exerted. An invisible energy was coming off her, consuming Nat so fully that her own eyes watered. Everlee reached across and slid her delicate touch over Nat's fingers, draped over her own knee. Everlee took that hand in a warm caress, then brought it to her supple lips.

Nat's heart was pounding. Desire inhabited every cell, seized every sense. Everlee reached for Nat's cheek. The touch was slow, and delicate, her eyes no less caressing of the contours of Nat's plain features, as if they were something so beautiful and precious.

Nat's whisper was trembling. "Please, Ev, make love to me."

Everlee's smiling reply thrilled her. As did the tender stroke of her jaw; as did the craving glance at her mouth; as did the proximity of Everlee's lips; as did Everlee's hot breath fusing with her own.

Everlee drifted into her, and Nat closed her eyes.

The first kiss was lingering, soft and yet powerful enough to reach Nat's belly.

The second was explosive, and reached every roused and rousing fibre.

Everlee's tongue met Nat's inside of a ravenous kiss that unleashed Nat's pent desire, and with it she caressed every inch of Everlee's clothed flesh, desperate to experience her naked; to taste every inch of her; to please every part of her.

Everlee slid her fingers along one side of Nat's neck, while she rained erotic affection on the other. Then those soft lips were at her lobe. "Come to the bedroom, my beautiful Walnut." They somehow made it to the bed – naked and ablaze – where Everlee granted Nat's request in a manner anything but frivolous, with a passion she had never experienced.

Four

Nat woke up at 05.03 to Everlee filling a suitcase. The smell of coffee filled the room, and the space was dimly lit with just the glow of the bedside lamp.

Nat sat up, drawing Everlee's attention, as well as her affection. The woman came and sat by her side, cupped Nat's cheeks and kissed her lips. Then she said, "I made you coffee."

Nat clutched Everlee's fingers and whispered, "Please don't go."

Everlee's smile drained. "This was the deal, my beautiful Walnut."

Nat didn't want to argue. But the quelling of it forced her eyes to water, and her throat to close. Everlee looked away. Then she stood and placed her hands on her hips. Then she ran a palm over her scalp. Then she sat again and clasped Nat's hands. "I want you to understand something. My leaving is... it's something I have to do, it's not something I want."

"Why can't I call you?"

"I'll be unreachable, at least for a while. But listen, when I can, I'll make contact. Okay?"

"How long?"

"I... I can't answer that, Walnut. I know it seems unfair, and if you'd rather not hear from me because of that, I understand."

Nat brushed Everlee's cheeks and replied, "I don't care how long it takes. I'll wait. I'll hate it, but I'll wait."

They kissed. Then Everlee said, "I've only got thirty minutes. I better get moving. You don't have to hurry. Just lock up on your way out. Okay?"

Nat nodded. The words *I love you* were on the tip of her tongue, but she swallowed them. It had only been three weeks, after all. Could a person fall in love in three weeks?

True to her word and thirty minutes later, Everlee Bertrand was gone.

Five

Monday, April 3.

My dearest Walnut,

At this moment I'm lying in a hospital bed, awaiting surgery. Of course, any surgery is risky, but this one, the doctors say, is particularly problematic. I know I should be concerned with that, but all I can think about is you.

I should never have allowed what happened between us. I was selfish, I know that. But you weren't the only one admiring from a distance. Perhaps I should be, but I'm not ashamed to say I have enjoyed every moment with you. If you're angry with me, my darling, know that you have every right to be. But I do hope you'll forgive me some day.

I'm hoping I can reveal all of this to you in person. I want to believe I'll be home soon, knocking on your door. I want to be able to tell you about the tumour, about how they successfully removed it from my cauliflower brain. I want to be able to tell you I'm fully recovered, and that I'm in love with you and so much want to be with you. I want that more than anything. But if you've received this letter, it means I didn't survive.

I'm so, so sorry, my dearest Nat. I never, ever wanted to hurt you. I know you'll move on and not waste a single moment of this precious life. I know you'll fill it with love, just as you've filled mine.

I love you, Walnut: my fantastic truth that no future darkness will diminish, that no further revelation will upend.

Yours. Always. Ev.

Thursday, April 6.

The post-lady popped the envelope in the slot, then rushed to the next one. Her load was large, and it was going to be a very, *very* long day.

3

*Write a story about someone who receives – or makes
– a life-changing, anonymous donation.*

THE HORSES

In her crisp white coat and with her dark hair pulled into a bun, Doctor Bailey peered over her black-rimmed specs. Brenda sat across from her, in a room at the hospital set up much like any other office Brenda had visited.

Doctor Bailey tilted the screen in Brenda's direction. "You see this?" She tapped the monitor with a pen. "This is your left kidney."

Brenda scanned the monochrome image. "Why doesn't it look like the right one?"

"Because it's shrivelled like a dried up old prune. It's functioning at about two percent of what it should be."

"I don't understand."

"It's possibly congenital. And your numbers are fine. But essentially you only have one kidney."

"But…"

Doctor Bailey sat back in her chair and threw her glasses on the desk. She sighed and rubbed her eyes. "You are so young, Brenda. You have a lot of living to do yet. I *am* sorry. I know you wanted to do this for her."

"But the blood tests. You said…"

"You *are* compatible. But, sweetheart, you don't have a kidney to give."

Uncomfortable with presenting – or feeling – any kind of emotion, Brenda swallowed the ones she was having into her gullet, and brushed her mousy hair behind her ear. "Okay."

"I wish I had better news."

Not one for words, Brenda simply nodded. She stood and walked to the door, then turned. "She doesn't know anything about this, right?"

"If there's one thing a doctor understands, it's discretion. I haven't breathed a word, Scout's honour."

Brenda gave another nod, then exited.

* * *

Brenda sat outside Macy's hospital room. With her head lolled against the wall, she gave it an angry shake. Brenda Ashton was not a good person. She knew it, because she didn't believe people could really be *good*. They were mostly selfish, ultimately treacherous, and therefore impossible to trust. It's what she believed of most people, herself included. Maybe it was because of her mother. Brenda's father had died when she was nine, and her memories of life before he got sick were... well, better than what came after. Her mother was a factory worker who had, since that dreadful day, drank herself to sleep every other night. Brenda had basically raised *herself*. When Lindy died in 2018 from alcohol poisoning, Brenda went to stay with her Aunt Carol. Aunt Carol was her mother's sister, and she insisted:

'Don't be angry with your mother, Bren. It wasn't the booze that killed her. She never did recover from the death of Clay. Those two were made for each other. When you find the one person in the world you're meant to be with, and they're taken away from you... well, for some, there's no coming back from that. Your mother died of a broken heart, plain and simple.'

If it were true, then death seemed to Brenda to be remarkably inefficient. If her father's demise by cancer were not considered slow by normal standards, then most assuredly her mother's broken heart – endured over almost a decade – must be. Then there was Macy.

Macy had been on the ward for her stupid busted kidneys, and Brenda wound up there for (stupidly enough) alcohol poisoning, which unlike her mother was *not* her fault, but the fault of her stupid stalker who had laced her drink with Rohypnol. Of course, no charges had been laid, because, *pfft*, patriarchy. Since then, she always carried a dagger in her boot, and she had every intention of using it if Jacob or anyone like him ever came near her again. She fully expected she'd be in jail before the year was out.

Since Brenda had known her, Macy had most always had a book in her hand. But she didn't have a book with her on that first fateful encounter. It didn't matter though. Macy recited poetry to her from memory, written by some dead fellow named Alfred something. Oh, Noyes. The Highwayman. Brenda never cared a lick for poetry, but Macy – unlike Brenda – did have a way with words, and she reeled them off that day in a manner that Brenda found... enchanting.

And so they became friends. Since then, Brenda had spent a lot of time at the hospital. But she never resented it. Not the smell. Not the sickness. Not the beeping of machines or constant flapping about of doctors and nurses. Not once did she resent the inconvenience of being friended to a person who could never go horse riding with her, or road tripping with her, or strolling the beach with her, or that thing she had imagined sometimes but would never, ever say. Right now, though, resentment was bubbling like a cauldron of filth, and the lid was rattling.

Nurse Yasmin stirred Brenda from her brooding. "Are you going in, darlin'? I know she's been waiting for you."

Brenda nodded, and Nurse Yasmin continued in her shuffle down the corridor. Brenda stood, sucked in a breath, fixed her hair, then walked into the room.

The twenty-two year old Macy was sitting up in bed, hooked to a machine. She was reading with eyes sunken like golf holes. Her skin was grey like nimbus clouds, but when Macy looked up and saw Brenda standing there, her face lit like daisies reaching for the sun.

"Beautiful Bee, come to me, in these hours that fill me with joy."

She always does this. Why does she always do this? Why does she insist on acting like the world is some goddam bleeding love poem? And that smile. It was a treacherous, tempting smile that conspired with the devil in its deceit.

Disgusting words swelled inside her, rancid as dead clams rotting in their shells, and Brenda unleashed them. "I *hate* you."

Macy's outstretched hand retraced, delicately returned to the folds of that vapid white blanket. With hostility barely contained, Brenda circled the room to the window. From behind the grey the sun drove its gay streams, and Brenda resented them too. More than the machines, more than the gowns, more than these goddam horizontal blinds. She looked down at the parking lot, and the cars blurred into lurid rainbow blobs.

She turned on Macy and hissed, "I wish I'd never met you."

There was a strain in Macy's jaw that precipitated streaks of sadness over those ashen cheeks, and they dripped off her unmoving chin. The next words that came to Brenda made her own jaw quiver for their vileness. But she couldn't stop them. "I hope you know I won't be sad if you die. I won't care."

Macy fiddled with the blanket at her lap. "Okay," she murmured. They stared at each other across the room, silent in their misery.

Macy broke eye contact. She sniffed and opened the book that Brenda had bought for her – Anna Sewell's Black Beauty. She said, "I had a dream about you last night." She laid her head back and stared at the ceiling. "We were riding bareback on two beautiful horses. Yours was a stunning black beast, and you raced ahead with your silky locks flowing behind you. I was on a palomino. As hard as I tried, I couldn't catch you. You were laughing, and I was too. I desperately wanted to reach you. I had something important to say, and I kept shouting at you to stop, but you just kept laughing and racing, and I was giddy with happiness."

Brenda's armour threatened to buckle, and she loped to the bed. Macy turned her an eye-popping fright, and Brenda yelled, "Stop this! You hear me? Stop it!"

Macy whispered, "Stop what?"

"Stop acting like you're not afraid. Stop acting like you think this is some goddam fairy-tale! No claret-dressed bad boy is gonna ride up on some goddam steed and whisk you away. No one is coming to save you!"

"Bee—"

"No!" Brenda pulled away.

Macy latched onto her hand. "Bee."

Brenda wasn't sure what she was seeing in those hollowed hazel eyes. "Why are you looking at me like that?"

"Like what? Like I love you?"

Brenda's throat choked shut. Her stomach twisted as if a tiny imp inside of her was gleefully fashioning a rope from her entrails. Old grief came flooding back, and she couldn't help wishing it would sink her.

Macy threw the covers aside, exposing a thinned frame under a dreary hospital gown. "Come on. Let me read to you."

Brenda's tirade had fizzled, as if suddenly the demon inside of her had been exorcised. She tried to speak, but shame allowed only one word to blubber out of her. "*Mace.*"

Macy reached a hand. "It's okay."

"I'm sorry."

"It's okay. Come."

Brenda wiped her sodden cheeks, then climbed onto the bed. She snuggled in, and was enveloped in a warm embrace she didn't deserve. Macy kissed Brenda's crown, then recounted Black Beauty's tale to the end.

* * *

Forty-eight hours later, a miracle happened. A kidney was found for the ailing Macy, who was barely lucid enough to register the news.

Doctor Bailey leaned over her and said, "We're prepping you for surgery, Macy. Everything's going to be okay."

By her side was Macy's mother, who gripped her hand. "We're right here, sweetheart. We'll be here when you wake up. You're going to be fine."

"Where is Bee? Is she here?"

"You don't need to worry about anything. We love you, sweetheart. We'll see you soon."

As they wheeled Macy away, she craned her neck to her mother. "Does Bee know? Will you tell her what's happening?"

"Everything's going to be okay, baby. You're going to get well. We love you so much."

* * *

Several hours prior to the operation…

Brenda snuck into Doctor Bailey's office and gently closed the door. She sat cross-legged in the middle of the room, then took the phone from her breast pocket. Doctor Bailey had been kind enough to share her private number, but Brenda had never had cause to use it. Until today. She called and pressed the phone to her ear.

"Hello, this is Monica."

"Doctor Bailey?"

"Hmm, that sounds like Brenda."

"Yeah. Yeah, it's Brenda."

"Is everything alright, sweetheart?"

"Are you at the hospital today?"

"I am. I'm just finishing up my rounds. Do you need to see me?"

"Can you be at your office in five minutes?"

"Of course. I'll head over now."

"I've left a note on your desk, but I trust you'll know what to do when you get here."

Brenda terminated the call.

She thought about her father; the life she knew before.

She thought about Lindy and her broken heart.

She imagined Macy, riding bareback on a palomino, giddy with happiness.

She took the dagger from her boot.

Then she stuck it in her neck.

4

Write about a character unknowingly experiencing a "sliding doors" moment. Write your story in two halves; what could have been, and what actually happened.

MY LITTLE CAGE

One

April 20, 2023
Thursday.

I don't want you to think I'm crazy. But the truth is, I see dead people. Not in a Haley Joel Osment/Bruce Willis kind of way, exactly...

Thirty-year-old Sydney Shepheard walked out of her psychologist's office into a sunny afternoon, having *not* said those words. Maybe her sessions with Doctor Sinclair were privileged, but that didn't mean she wanted to give him a reason to recommend a stay at Crystal Waters, the mental institution two sleepy towns over.

Feeling unsettled, Sydney decided on a guaranteed pick-me-up. The business district was small and everything close, the bank only a 300-metre stroll down the main street. As well, the weather couldn't have been more pleasant for a Tasmanian autumn day.

Kristelle was behind the counter, shielded from the outside world by a pane of Perspex. While Sydney waited her turn, she appreciated the twenty-nine-year-old's air. She wore a crisp, powder-blue shirt, her long burgundy mane was tied in a charmingly messy knot, and the cobalt frames of her specs conveyed to Sydney a delightful spark of spirit.

As Kristelle snapped a rubber band around a wad of fifties, she caught Sydney's eye and winked as she handed the cash to the gent she was serving.

Sydney's heart fluttered.

The man thanked Kristelle and departed, and Sydney fixed an imagined stray fringe as she stepped to the counter.

Kristelle beamed. "Good afternoon, Miss Shepheard."

"Good afternoon, Miss Kent."

"How does your day progress?"

"Great, actually. I made it through another appointment without being committed."

Kristelle chuckled. "I knew you could do it." They exchanged a smile, which left Sydney evidently stupid. Kristelle said, "Well, tell me, Miss Shepheard, what is it I can do for you today? Let me guess, you've got your eye on the new two dollar."

"A roll of ones, if you would be so kind."

"What is it you hope to get your hands on *this* time?"

"Two-thousand-twenty *Donation* coin. You can't miss it. It has a green middle. I'm a sucker for green on gold."

"Ah. Well, I'll keep an eye out." Kristelle opened the drawer with a wry smile on her lips. "Surely there's an easier way to acquire these coins, dear Syd."

"Easier maybe, but nowhere near as fun."

"Like Charlie finding his golden ticket inside a Wonka bar?"

"Exactly."

Kristelle pushed the roll through the slot. On seeing Kristelle's hand safely retrace, Sydney reached for the tightly packed cylinder... only to spot Kristelle's hand returning and apparently reaching for Sydney's own.

Sydney recoiled. Kristelle snapped her hand back, and the weightless smile vanished. In its place was pink-cheeked embarrassment. She smoothed her hands over the bodice of her shirt. "I'm... I'm sorry, Syd."

Shamed, Sydney murmured, "No, Krissy, *I'm* sorry. It's... it's not..."

Kristelle peered over Sydney's shoulder. "I... I need to keep serving. Don't want to upset the boss."

"Maybe... maybe I'll see you tomorrow if... if I strike out with this lot."

"I won't be in. It's my day off."

"Oh."

Before Sydney turned, Kristelle said, "I'll be in Monday though, if you're still chasing your green on gold."

At least partially relieved, Sydney gave her a thin smile before shuffling to the exit.

Two

Sunday afternoon relinquished the charm of its earlier hours, with a cloud cover that wasn't quite a blanket, but thick enough to keep the temperature on the chillier side of agreeable.

Even so, Sydney ventured out to the park, and took a seat there with a book. She could have devoured its pages in the heated comfort of her apartment, but it was too quiet there. Out here she had her green in the Blackwood and Eucalypt, and the pink of galah's fossicking in the grass. She had families walking dogs and pushing strollers, holding hands and stroking backs. Although Sydney wouldn't allow herself to be touched, she still needed the presence of people: their easy laughter, their mundane chatter, their own physical connection that somehow appeased Sydney's lack of it, even from a distance.

A burst of sunshine brightened the page, and then a shadow fell across it. Sydney looked up to find Kristelle smiling down at her. "Miss Shepheard. It's... it's nice to see you outside the confines of my little cage."

Sydney was seized by a moment of dread. But she quickly realised that after the episode at the bank, Kristelle would unlikely try to touch her again. She sucked in a breath, then offered a warm, "Hello, Miss Kent."

"Do you mind if I join you?"

The bench was generously sized, affording Sydney some comfort. "I don't mind."

Kristelle sat at the end. Sydney studied her with a smile. The hue of Krissy's spectacles made her blue eyes all the more vibrant, and her voluminous hair fell freely over her shoulders.

Kristelle's hands stayed in her pockets as she said, "Listen, about what happened—"

"I am... so sorry about that. I didn't mean to offend you."

Kristelle gave a shallow nod. "I guess I... I guess I thought maybe you were coming to the bank to see me. It was presumptuous. I made you uncomfortable and I'm sorry."

Sydney wanted to explain. So badly, she wanted to justify her behaviour. Kristelle removed a fist from her pocket. She unfurled it to reveal a pristine gold coin, with a sphere of green at its centre. "I... I found this just this morning. You wouldn't believe, it came with the change from my coffee. I thought I'd give it to you Monday, but here we are." She offered up the gift with an open palm.

There was no way Sydney could accept it without touching Kristelle's skin. She looked into a kind expression with profound regret, only to see those eyes fall with matching disappointment. Kristelle laid the coin on the seat between them, and then stood.

Sydney said, "Wait, Krissy. Don't... don't go. Please. Let me explain." Kristelle's tautness of jaw indicated to Sydney not annoyance, but concern. She sat, and Sydney checked over her shoulder for ears that might have been too close. Then she said, "I don't want you to think I'm a complete nut job."

"Okay. No assumptions about jobs – nutty or otherwise – will be made." Kristelle pointed three fingers skyward and joined her thumb and pinkie. "Scout's honour."

Sydney grimaced for the thought of saying what she was about to say. "Sometimes... sometimes I see things."

Kristelle waited on a stroller to pass them by, then muttered, "*See things? Syd, I don't...*"

"When I touch people."

Kristelle ran a sharp eye over her. "Or when people touch *you*."

Sydney nodded glumly.

"What kinds of things do you see?"

Sydney sighed. "Sickness. Disease. And sometimes – I know this sounds insane – sometimes I see death." Kristelle's right eyebrow bounced harder than a Djokovic serve. Sydney groaned. "You think I'm crazy."

"No." Sydney cocked her incredulous noodle. Kristelle responded, "Well, maybe I was getting there. But I'm not there yet." Sydney sighed and tried to sink further into the seat. All she succeeded in doing was hurting her backbone. Kristelle asked sincerely, "Explain it to me. What does sickness look like?"

"It's... it's hard to describe."

"Take your time."

The last time it had happened was after a contact between Sydney and a co-worker, who had patted her on the shoulder. The image was chiselled into her brain like David into stone. "Melty, I guess. Like wax over flame."

Kristelle asked solemnly, "They look like that all the time?"

"No. Just a... it's just a moment. Then they appear normal again."

"And what about death? What does death look like?"

The sun disappeared behind a cloud, and the temperature dropped so rapidly that Sydney shivered. She hugged herself and replied, "Grey. Dark. Empty."

"How do you know it means what you think it means? Everybody gets sick eventually, Syd. Everybody dies."

"Not like this. It doesn't take long once I've seen it. A couple of months. Sometimes it's only a matter of days."

"So, it doesn't happen every time you touch someone?"

"I don't know anymore. I haven't touched anyone in a very long time."

"How long?"

Sydney sat forward and clasped her hands. "That last time, I was leaving on a plane for Melbourne. My family – my parents and two sisters – dropped me off at the airport. As we were saying goodbye, I saw it in all their faces. This grey... *nothing*. I was so scared. Before that day, I had only seen sickness. But I knew. Somehow, I knew something terrible was going to happen. All four of them died in a car accident the next day. That was eight years ago, and I haven't touched anyone since."

After a long, silent stare at the ground, Sydney sat back and looked over at her company. Kristelle's lids were like overwrought dams, and they were buckling under the strain.

"Oh, Syd. I'm... I'm so sorry."

With her own eyes watering, Sydney said, "I never gave a damn about coins until you started working at that bank. But I wanted an excuse to come and see you. And I thought it was safer that way because..."

"Because of the barrier." Sydney nodded. Kristelle inched closer, triggering Sydney's alarm. Kristelle stalled with palms raised. She said, "Well, maybe... maybe it's not something to be afraid of. Maybe it's a warning system. Maybe you can share what you see."

"But I don't know how it's going to happen. There isn't enough there to be useful."

"Okay. Okay, let's put it to the test."

"What?" Kristelle offered a paw, and Sydney replied with a vigorous headshake.

Kristelle said gently, "Come on."

"No. I... I can't."

"Listen to me. You did not cause the death of your family. They are not gone because of anything you saw or did. And if you see that I'm sick, or that my own demise is near, maybe it's something I can change."

Sydney implored, "But I... I don't want to see you that way. *Ever*."

"Well, what *I* want is to touch you. I want to touch you, Syd Shepheard. And I'm sure as hell not going to let you go another eight years without you touching someone else."

"I... Krissy, I can't."

Kristelle slid her butt across the seat. She brought herself so close that Sydney was sure she could feel the heat radiating from Kristelle's flesh. Without touching, Kristelle made a gesture of cupping Sydney's jaw. Her fingers were so near, Sydney froze for fear of inadvertently bumping into them. She was frightened, but she was also enthralled. She hadn't seen eyes this close for what felt like an eternity, and the intricate patterns of Kristelle's irises appeared as nothing short of a masterpiece.

Her heart jacked in her chest like billiard balls slamming the cushion. She had no idea if it was fear, or excitement, or a rousing blend of both.

Kristelle murmured, "I'm going to kiss you now, Syd, just so you know." The only way out was to fall off the edge of the seat. But Sydney didn't want to fall off the edge.

Instead, she whispered, "I... I guess I can't stop you."

Kristelle flashed a smile. Sydney closed her eyes. Kristelle's fingertips – warm and gentle – stroked the underneath of Sydney's jaw. Then those soft, full lips pressed against her mouth. At first, Sydney was just a tactile witness to the supple flesh that connected with her own. But then she was a willing participant, oblivious to anything that wasn't Kristelle Kent. The warmth of her. The clean, coconut scent of her. The tenderness of each impeccably crafted caress.

When that magic kiss ended, and without opening her eyes, Sydney found Kristelle's cheek.

Kristelle whispered, "Look at me, Syd. Don't be afraid."

Sydney gulped a cool breath. Then she slowly peeled her eyes.

Kristelle was looking back at her, vibrant and whole. "Tell me, what do you see?"

Sydney could barely contain her joy. She pulled Kristelle into an ecstatic hug, and Kristelle returned it with laughing glee.

Three

Two years later.

Sydney returned home at 18:38 Friday night, to the aroma of basil and garlic.

Kristelle was in the kitchen, hovering over the stove. Without turn of head, she said, "Honey, where on earth have you been? Gemma and Patty will be here any minute. Dinner is almost ready. I think it just needs a little more..." She doused the open pan with salt from the grinder.

Sydney stepped in close behind her. "There's something I need to tell you."

Kristelle glanced over her shoulder, and on detecting Sydney's earnestness, switched off the stove. She turned and gently palmed Sydney's cheek. "What is it? Did... has something happened? Oh, god, Syd. Did you see something? You haven't seen anything this whole—"

Noting the worry in her eyes, Sydney took the small velvet gift box from her pocket. "I did see something. I saw *you*. I didn't want to see anybody. I didn't want to feel this way. I was so scared of what it would mean. You saved me from that misery. I thought I was crazy, but you never treated me as anything other than unique. I can't imagine where I'd be without you today, and I cannot imagine my life without you going forward. Kristelle Kent, will you do me the honour of accepting this very expensive ring?"

The misty-eyed Kristelle patted her chest, then removed the diamond-adorned hoop from its nest. She was beaming when she said, "Well now, that depends. Can you reschedule Gemma and Patty in the next five minutes? Because I have an urge to do very smutty things to you right now."

"Oh, about that. Gemma called earlier. They can't make it till eight."

Kristelle slid the ring on her finger, then slipped her arms around Sydney's neck. "Then it will be my privilege to accept this very expensive ring." They shared a kiss. Slow. Deep. Then Kristelle murmured, "Dear Syd, you are my green on gold, the love of my life. Please come with me to the bedroom where I will do very smutty things to you."

Sydney reached for the pan, and put the lid on dinner.

Four

April 20, 2023
Thursday

Sydney sat in the tidy, if not cosy, office of her psychologist, Peter Sinclair. Across from her was a grand landscape photo, perhaps as much as two metres wide, of a rocky beach, with a lone seagull at its centre.

The balding, business-shirted Peter said, "This is your safe place, Sydney. You know we can talk about anything. There is no right or wrong here."

Sydney picked at her sleeve. So often she'd thought about telling him, and yet had chickened out every time. She knew how it sounded. It *sounded* insane. But he was a doctor. Surely, he'd fielded admissions *way* crazier.

She picked up the half empty glass in front of her and sipped. Then she took a deep breath and expelled a confession. "I don't want you to think I'm crazy. But the truth is, I... I see *dead* people. Not in a Haley Joel Osment/Bruce Willis kind of way, exactly..."

At the end of the session, Doctor Peter Sinclair would recommend Sydney voluntarily commit herself to a stint at Crystal Waters. After having not allowed herself the touch of another human being for the past eight years, her delusions were having a very real, very negative impact on her life.

Sydney would leave his office, and decide against visiting the bank. Clearly, she was ill and needed to get herself well, instead of fantasizing about Kristelle and the kind of relationship the two of them might have.

Sydney would spend six months at Crystal Waters. In that time, she would be medicated and counselled, and still fall into depression on leaving. She would not be cured, and Kristelle Kent would become nothing more than a dreamy respite from a foggy, drug-induced hell.

Sydney would live another eight years, and die alone of a prescription-drug overdose.

The only thing of value to be retrieved from her residence will be an extensive coin collection, and with *that*, a photo of a smiling burgundy-haired woman, wearing cobalt-rimmed specs.

5

Your protagonist walks past an intriguing stranger, then turns around to take another look at them. The stranger turns around too. Write about what happens next.

THE ENTHUSIASTIC TAIL OF THE Z

The Accident.

I n the tight squeeze of the goodie-crammed craft shop, Beth took a set of art brushes and four tubes of acrylic to the counter. She was greeted with the creaseless, creeping smile of Grace Mann, an athletic brunette with twelve years less on her bones.

"Good morning, Beth. I love the new cut. Very chic."

Beth ran a hand over the short hairs at the back of her head, the premature salt-n-pepper of her velvety crop. "It's taken some getting used to."

"It looks great. How does it feel to be forty?"

Beth took the debit card from the pocket of her full-length black coat. "It feels like a good age to be moving to a warmer climate."

Grace chuckled. "Knees a bit creaky?"

"Knees and knuckles are the first to go, I'm told."

"Gah. Will we see you at Heather's tonight?"

"I don't think so. I'm in the middle of a really good book."

Grace coupled an emphatic sigh with a condemning eye. "You're not going to meet Mrs Right that way, you know."

"I've met *several* Mrs Rights that way."

"Beth, you need to switch the CLOSED sign to OPEN. There is someone out there for you. But they aren't just going to fall into your lap. Believe me, I know."

Beth chortled. "Billy Thorn?"

"Ugh. Don't remind me."

"What if I'm dating Mrs Wrong when Mrs Right comes along?"

"That is an excuse for procrastination, Bethany Duncan."

"Alright. You know what the difference between the two of us is,

Grace?"

"You mean besides the fact I don't have a single grey hair and my boobs are perkier than a cheerleader on crack?"

"Aside from that. I like my own company. I'd rather be alone than share my time with someone who is going to scratch my LP's and eat all the pepitas."

"Pepitas? Darling, you really do need to get out more. How ya gonna find someone if you spend all your time alone? Come to Heather's tonight."

Despite her protest, Beth couldn't deny a longing, or a loneliness. Not that she expected it to be filled by a night out at Heather's. "I'll think about it."

"Leave the pumpkin seeds at home. Believe me, nobody wants them. That'll be seventy-two dollars for the supplies. The cheery demeanour and worldly advice are free."

Beth stepped out of the shop's lilac-scented air into a chilly breeze. She shoved her purchases into her pockets and headed north past the optometrist and the Indian restaurant. At the traffic lights, she pressed the button and waited. The lights changed, the alert pinged, and the little green man indicated the time for loitering was over.

The small beachside town had a population of under 10,000, and Beth had lived there for the past twelve years. As a result, the faces coming at her from the opposite direction were mostly familiar. Except for one stand-out: a blonde woman in perhaps her late thirties, with a hand shoved deep into the pocket of her long mauve coat. In heels, she outpaced the others, tackling a wild strand that had been caught in a violent gust.

She brushed past. Beth stopped and turned. The woman arrived at the other side, but with a significantly slowed step. She stopped outside the restaurant, and as the other pedestrians passed her, she pivoted.

Their eyes connected, and something inexplicable transpired. Beth couldn't fathom in that moment the feeling she was having. and the woman looked back at Beth with eyes that appeared just as mystified. But then those eyes were alarm. Those eyes were fright. The woman thrust a palm towards Beth and shouted, "*No!*" It was the last thing Beth knew before the squealing of tyres, the snapping of bones, the feeling of flight, and her skull cracki—

The Coma.

Three weeks later...

It was 20:52 on a Wednesday evening. The hospital room was

dimly lit when Mackenzie Gregor parked her backside in the chair by Bethany's side. The coma meant that Bethany needed to be tube-fed, but she was breathing on her own, which could only be a positive sign.

Mackenzie took Bethany's hand and stroked it, as Bilbo might stroke his 'precious'. "Hey there. It's me again. Mackenzie. It's outside visiting hours, but your mum talked the nurses into letting me stay. She's really very nice. She's told me all about you. Betty is very proud of her girl." As per every one of Mackenzie's visits, Bethany remained unresponsive. Mackenzie stood and leaned over the patient, brushed a hand over her forehead. "Listen, I'm afraid I have to go. I hate leaving you like this, but I was never supposed to be here this long."

Mackenzie sat and sighed. What *was* she still doing here? She had a job. She had responsibilities. She had a cat that was currently in the care of her best friend, who hated cats and had messaged every day for Mackenzie to get her arse back home to her troublemaking feline familiar.

Mackenzie touched Bethany's arm. "What are we doing here, Beth? Why were you stopped in the middle of the street? I know that driver ran a red light, but you would've made it across if you'd just kept walking. So, what were you doing? Please tell me."

Mackenzie had lived the episode on repeat since it had happened. When she wasn't overwhelmed by the sickening crunch of the car slamming into Bethany's legs, or by the horrifying vision of the woman being hurled like a broken Barbie, she was consumed by the strange feeling that had overtaken her in those seconds after first seeing Beth in the street. What had compelled Mackenzie to turn around? Why was Beth looking back at her with a mirrored sense of wonder? Would the accident have been avoided had Mackenzie not been there? And why was Mackenzie finding it so difficult to walk away when she had already done everything she could to help a perfect stranger?

Mackenzie's phone rang. It was Derek, Mackenzie's ex-boyfriend. They had been split since before her trip, but he was still harassing her; still unable to take no for an answer. Mackenzie terminated the call and reluctantly got to her feet. She leaned over the bed and brought her nose to within inches of Beth's.

"I have to go now, Beth. But I know you're going to be okay. You'll wake up when you're good and ready, and your family will be here for you. I've left my number with your mum, so that if you want, you can reach me. I don't want you to feel as though you have to, but I really hope you call." Mackenzie caressed Beth's cheek and kissed it. It occurred to her that perhaps she shouldn't have, but it felt like the most natural thing in the world. It didn't feel as though she were kissing a stranger. It felt as though...

She whispered, "I know you're in there, Bethany. If you can hear me, please wake up. Wake up and ask me to stay. Or wake up and ask me to leave. Just please, wake up."

Mackenzie waited. There was no beat of Bethany's lashes. No twitch of her cheek. No tremor of her lip.

Mackenzie let go Beth's hand. "Goodbye, Beth." As wrong as it felt, she turned away. As queasy as her gut, she walked out of the room. As much as her jaw quivered, she continued down the corridor, not knowing why it hurt, only knowing that it did.

Twenty minutes later, Bethany stirred.

Two hours later, Bethany woke.

The Last Thing I Remember.

Bethany's white-haired, spec-wearing mother beamed and wept with joy. "Oh, my baby."

"Mum."

Betty kissed her daughter's crown. "I knew you'd come back to us."

"The doctor... she said there was an accident?"

Betty sat down with her hands wrapped around Beth's. "You don't remember?"

"No. No, I've tried, but..."

"Honey, you were struck by a car at the traffic lights on King Edward."

"The last thing I remember is... is Grace Mann. I was talking to her at the shop, I think."

"That's right, honey. You'd just left there when the accident happened. You were crossing the street and a driver ran a red light."

All Bethany could see was Grace. The only word that came to her was *pepitas.*

Betty said, "It doesn't matter, my baby. You came back to us. That's all I care about."

After a lengthy discussion with the doctor about rehabilitation, Betty opened the bag at her feet. She pulled out a sketch pad and Bethany's art pencils. "Here you go. I thought you could use these while you're here; keep yourself occupied."

"Is my phone here?"

"Oh, of course, honey." Betty slid open the top drawer by the bed. "These are the things you had on you. The paramedics returned them."

Inside was Beth's phone, surprisingly intact considering what Beth had been told about the accident. Also, a set of paint brushes and four tubes of Liquitex acrylic paint: Iridescent white; Light pink; Cadmium yellow; Deep violent. Bethany took up the violet, momentarily mesmerised. She returned the tube to the drawer and swung the table over her legs. She opened the sketch pad and placed it, portrait-style, on the surface. Then she took up a pencil.

"Oh," said Betty. "You wanna do this now?"

Bethany touched lead to paper, and as if by magic, an image formed in her mind.

The Portrait.

After a fevered two hours, the rough portrait was done. First, a pencil drawing. Then a palette improvised from a dish Nurse Stanton had kindly supplied. A touch of iridescent white swirled through a splash of violet. Then a drawing embellished with acrylic. A sweep of mauve here, a stroke of yellow there, and a dash of pink at the lips.

Bethany contemplated the image, as though by sheer will she could breathe life into it.

Betty entered the room after ducking out for dinner. "Okay. Show me."

Beth held up the A3 leaf.

Betty said, "Oh, honey. That's Mackenzie Gregor."

"I... I don't..."

Betty sat down and pulled the chair close. She touched Beth's hand. "She was with you at the accident. She called for the ambulance. You'd stopped breathing at the scene, honey, so she gave you CPR until the paramedics arrived."

Beth studied the portrait, and wandered how it was she had summoned the image without recalling a memory.

Betty further explained, "She was over for work and was supposed to fly home that day, but she stayed so that she could come visit you. She sat and chatted with you many times."

Beth asked earnestly, "Why?"

"I know the two of you hadn't met, but from the concern she showed for you, it was hard to believe." Betty searched her bag. She withdrew a slip of paper and opened it, then palmed it to Beth. "She said you could call if you wanted, but that she would understand if you didn't."

Beth studied the distinct handwriting: the emphatic arches of the M, the bold swirl of the *a*, the enthusiastic tail of the Z. She murmured, "Mackenzie Gregor saved my life."

Betty swallowed and nodded. "Yes, my darling. She did."

The Number.

Later, after Beth assured her mother that she was fine but needed some rest, Betty left her alone. Beth took the note from the drawer, and also her phone which Betty had thought to charge.

Beth unlocked the device, brought up the keypad and punched in the number. Then with a certain level of anxiety, she hit the green icon.

She brought the phone to her lobe.

'The number you have called is not connected. Please check the number and try again.'

Beth tried a second time, for the same result.

A Memory I Don't Remember Having.

Twelve months later...

Bethany was in the studio at the back of her small Penguin gallery. Penguin was a tiny-but-growing coastal town only ten kilometres west of Ulverstone, and the main street was right on the water. The day outside was wet, the sea animated. Not to be dissuaded, the doorbell jingled.

Bethany called, "Good morning."

A feminine voice replied, "Good morning."

"I'll be right out."

"No rush. I'm happy to browse."

Beth added a few more touches of teal, then dropped the brush in a cup of water. She grabbed her cane and limped out of the studio into the main gallery, where a woman stood in a hooded coat, gazing at a portrait not long hung.

The lady asked, "How much for this one?"

"Actually, that one's not for sale. I apologise. It should have been tagged as such."

"It's... it's very good."

"Thank you. I call it *Waiting*."

"*Waiting*," the woman repeated thoughtfully. She asked, "Why not for sale?"

Beth eyed the portrait, imperfect but superior to its predecessors. "It's my favourite."

"Intriguing. A likeness sharp enough to induce nostalgia, not *quite* enough to attach a name."

Beth nodded a regretful agreement. "She's a memory I don't remember having."

"I see. Perhaps you're not meant to remember."

"I can't believe that." Beth gazed wistfully at her own work, wishing she could do better. "She saved my life. I don't want the image to be vague. I want it to be crystal clear. I want her to know what she did for me. I wish I could tell her."

"Do you think gratitude is what she wants from you?"

"I don't know that she wants anything from me. Still…"

"She saved you." Bethany nodded. The woman said, "If you don't remember, how do you know? Perhaps it was you who saved her."

Beth took her eyes off the canvas and considered the woman's profile, hidden behind the hood. "I was hit by a car. I was broken. She kept me alive until the ambulance arrived. I was in a coma for three weeks and never saw her again. How could I have saved her?"

The woman faced her then, wearing mirrored shades. She dropped the hood and removed her glasses, and with them off, removed almost all doubt.

Almost all. "*Mackenzie?*"

Mackenzie Gregor revealed a set of stunning white teeth in a broad smile. "Bethany Duncan. It is… truly wonderful to finally meet you."

"I…" Beth peered up at the painting, then back at her muse.

Mackenzie herself looked to the portrait and said, "It really is a very good likeness, considering you only saw me for a few seconds. But I am not at all deserving, dear Beth."

On her cane, Beth hobbled closer. "I tried to call you, but the number you left was disconnected."

"I am *so* sorry about that. I was in trouble. But you *did* save me, Beth. Because of you, I didn't return home as expected. My ex assumed I *had* returned, and decided to take his pound of flesh. He broke into my garage and set my car on fire. The tank exploded and the house caught alight. Everything burned. Everything."

"God. Mackenzie, I'm… I'm so sorry."

"He's in prison now for arson, but I'm sure if I'd been there, he'd be serving time for murder."

"I'm so sorry you've been through that. But something tells me you are a formidable woman, Mackenzie Gregor. I prefer to think if you'd been there, you'd have stopped him."

Mackenzie stepped close. "Maybe. And maybe if I hadn't been there crossing paths with you that day, you wouldn't have been hit by a car."

"Mackenzie, I don't…" Beth was flooded then, by images as clear as they were profound. Memories that had so long been teetering on the edge of her consciousness, came sharply into focus. She remembered the paints in her pockets; the winter chill on her cheeks. She remembered waiting at the lights. She remembered passing Mackenzie in the street. She remembered the feeling that had welled so overwhelmingly inside of her. She remembered turning, she remembered the fright in Mackenzie's eyes before everything went dark.

Beth replied, "That… that's different."

"It's only different if I wasn't the reason you stopped on that road. Can you tell me that? That I wasn't the reason?"

Beth dropped her eyes. "No. No, I can't tell you that." She leaned her cane against the wall, then took Mackenzie's hands. Mackenzie's distraught features softened. Beth said, "But I can tell you this. I'm not sorry it happened."

Mackenzie whispered, "No?"

"No. I remember now. Something… something *changed* when I saw you. I can't explain it, and I won't deny it. I don't pretend to understand. I only know that up until that moment, I'd been waiting for something. But when I saw you that day, crossing the street in my tiny little town, somehow I knew the waiting was over."

Mackenzie brushed Beth's jaw with light fingers. "Yes. Yes, that's exactly how I felt, dear Beth. Like the waiting – the searching – was over. I don't understand it either. I only know it felt right. Being here with you feels *right*." Ecstatic that she wasn't alone in her feelings, Beth touched her forehead to Mackenzie's, and they shared a quiet moment.

Beth muttered, "So, what happens now, Mackenzie Gregor?"

"I honestly don't know. I've waited so long to meet you. And now that I'm finally here, I…"

"What? Tell me."

"I… I find myself wanting to kiss you. If it's too soon, if you want to wait…"

Beth tenderly stroked Mackenzie's chin. "Oh, I think I'm done waiting." Mackenzie bewitched with a smile, then drifted enticingly towards her. Their lips were almost touching when Beth whispered, "There is just *one* thing I need to do."

Mackenzie breathed, "Okay."

Beth slipped away, then limped to the door.

She smiled for what felt like pure joy, then switched the OPEN sign to CLOSED.

6

Write about two friends who were once inseparable, but now find themselves growing apart – or even friends turned to enemies.

THE UNBRACED HULL

S aturday, February 18, 2023

With the flick of a switch a darkness descended, prompting an abrupt silence. Harper Jenkins crouched low behind the couch, alert as a panther. The wall-mounted clock counted the quiet seconds before the *zip* of a key in the deadbolt, and its double cylinders clunking. *Click.* Warm light splashed from the three hanging orbs overhead, prompting Harper, Claudia, and thirty other guests to jump and holler, "Surprise!"

Annie Gardner almost leapt out of the sensible lace-up shoes that accompanied her navy-blue paramedic attire. She patted her chest, and her gaping mouth stretched into a beaming grin. With sparkling eyes, the auburn-haired thirty-four-year-old scanned the room and said, "Alright, well, I noticed a bunch of muddy boot prints on my nice clean footpath, so the police are on their way."

The strapping farm hand, Roger Everett, stuck his hand in the air. "That was me, sorry." Annie and the bubbly gathering laughed, and then they all swarmed to the birthday girl with their affection. Claudia, Harper's oldest friend, left her side to join them, while Harper herself stayed put. She watched with admiration as Annie became the subject of much hugging and fussing.

Soon after, Annie's favourite Foo Fighters album was blaring when the birthday girl found both Harper and Claudia in the crowd.

"Hey, Claude!" Annie and Claudia embraced, which to Harper's shame sparked a rush of jealousy.

Claudia said, "Happy birthday, beautiful."

"Thank you." The pair uncoupled, and Harper studied Annie's emerald eyes, which came to her with what Harper wished could be more than just friendship.

Harper said, "Happy birthday, Annie." Annie smiled and inched towards her. It was for a feeling of unworthiness that Harper folded her arms in front of her chest.

Annie rubbed her own forearm. "Thanks for coming, Harp. It's so good to see you; *both* of you. Work has been crazy. I feel like I've been neglecting everyone."

Harper said, "I'm sure that's not—"

Claudia blurted, "I've got something for you." Out of her handbag she pulled a pink envelope and passed it to Annie with obvious pride.

Annie said, "Claude, you didn't have to..." She drew from the envelope a slip, and her mouth fell open. "Claude, this is..."

Claudia said, "I admit to a little selfishness. I booked myself in, but I wanted someone to join me, and I knew you'd be super keen."

Annie didn't quite meet Harper's gaze when she said, "I can't imagine Harp would've turned you down."

Claudia replied, "She did, actually. Didn't you, Harp?"

Although Harper's loyalty was wearing catastrophically thin, she decided against embarrassing her *friend*, and remained silent instead of answering honestly.

Annie said, "Claudia, this is extremely generous. I..."

"Don't you dare say no. Come on. It'll be a blast."

Harper gauged Annie's expression. Her parted plum lips were neither smiling nor frowning, but rather stalled at the in-between. She then exhaled a breath of submission. "I'd love to. I've never jumped out of a plane before. It'll be an amazing experience. Thank you so much."

Harper threw a glare at Claudia. Excitement stirred in the woman's cheeks like two ripe tomatoes bursting through the skin.

Harper's modest gift for Annie was in her handbag, and thanks to Claudia's grand offering, in Harper's handbag it stayed.

Laney swooped in and looped her arm around her best friend's waist. "Annie. I've got another surprise for you, straight from the airport. Come and see!" Annie checked Harper with a glance indecipherable before Laney whisked her away into the crowd.

Harper turned on her *friend*, a term that meant less and less these days. "Really, Claude? Sky diving?" Claudia brushed curly dark locks off her shoulder. Then she took a sip of bourbon. Harper wanted to swipe the glass from her backstabbing fingers. "You knew I wanted to do this for her. You knew I couldn't afford it right now and you..." Over Claudia's shoulder Harper caught sight of Annie, who looked back at her with what might have been concern. Harper feigned a smile and turned.

Claudia gulped down the rest of her beverage, then leaned close and whispered, "I'm sorry if you feel I'm treading on your toes, but I have a lot more in common with Annie than you do. And seriously, Harp, the last thing you should be worrying about in your current situation is a new relationship."

"Oh, so this is you doing me a favour."

"This is me going after what I want. Maybe if you'd done the same, you wouldn't be living in a tent in that god awful caravan park, and I wouldn't have to justify my friendship with a... with a bloody *vagrant*."

Harper's eyes stung for words she deemed both tactless and cruel. But Claudia wasn't done.

"Look at this place, Harp. Look at *her*. What can you and Annie *possibly* have in common? I'm saying this as a friend: don't embarrass yourself. You need to focus on the basics. You need to get your shit together. There. I said it. I'm going to get another drink."

Claudia left her there, with the music pumping, the crowd chattering, and Harper's tears ballooning.

Seeking solitude, Harper stepped out onto the balcony and leaned against the railing. It was dark out, and a pleasant breeze brushed her fringe across her brow. She peered out over the strait. The lights of passing ships glimmered like stars, cutting a slow but steady path through the night.

A gentle voice came from behind. "Here you are." Harper turned to Annie's warm smile. "I've been looking for you."

"I just needed some air. It's a beautiful evening."

Annie stood beside her and cast her eye out. "It certainly is." The smile diminished. "Listen, Harp, Claude told me about the house. I am so sorry that happened to you."

Not at all thrilled by Claudia's gossiping, Harper replied, "It's just temporary. I'll find something. I'll be okay."

"The market is insane right now. I'd offer you a room if I could. As it is, Laney's fella is moving in. They jacked up his rent, and he was already struggling. Is there anything I can do for you?"

"I'm fine. Really."

"Are you sure? I feel so awful."

"Please, don't. I'll be okay. I just... I just need to get my shit together."

"This isn't your fault, Harp. The housing crisis here is very real. You don't deserve to be without a home. *No one* deserves that."

Grateful for Annie's understanding, Harper took the package from her handbag. Still embarrassed by its modest value, she said, "Listen, I'm gonna get going soon, but I wanted to give this to you first. It's... it's nothing big. Happy birthday."

Annie's wide grin returned. "You didn't have to do that, Harp."

"It's not much, but I... I hope you like it."

Annie ripped into the red packaging with enthusiasm, and then her jaw dropped. She beheld Harper then, with eyes full of gratitude. "How ever did you find this?"

Harper's heart lifted. "It took a bit of tracking down, but I... well, I was determined."

The book – Given This Day – was written by Ree, an independent author who had self-published only two novels before she disappeared under what police had deemed 'suspicious circumstances.' Annie owned and adored the first book, but the second had been unpublished only weeks after its release, so that the few copies that had been printed were the only ones that would ever exist. Not only did Harper have to track one down, she had to offer five times the book's original asking price to entice the owner to sell.

Annie turned the tome in her hand and brushed delicate fingers over the glossy cover. Then she took Harper in her arms and gushed over her shoulder, "This is the most thoughtful gift I've ever received. Thank you so much, Harp."

After Claudia's scorn, Annie's kindness seemed all the more profound.

The glass door rumbled, and Laney stepped onto the balcony. "Am I interrupting?"

Annie let Harper go and replied, "We were just catching up."

Laney's sideways glance stirred Harper once more to shame; a discomfiture that wouldn't be undone by the brunette's cheery offering: "It's time to cut the cake."

Annie gave Harper a wink. "Come on. You have to at least stay for cake."

Laney dragged Annie away, and at the door looked back over her shoulder.

Harper imagined in that moment, what Laney and others might be saying about her. Harper without a home; Harper living in a tent; Harper with her low-paying job who was no doubt just one step away from the gutter.

Humiliated, Harper didn't stay for cake. Instead, she eased her way through the crowd, snuck through to the front door, and left without further word.

* * *

Laney dragged Annie into her bedroom and blustered, "Please tell me you're not thinking of dating that woman."

Annie's hackles rose. "Why? Because she's having a bit of a rough time right now?"

"What? No! I'm talking about Claudia Lyle."

"Oh." Annie rubbed the back of her neck. "Well, I... I get the impression she's interested."

"But are you interested in *her*?"

"We share some common ground, I suppose."

"That's not what I asked you."

Annie glanced down at the book in her hand. The spine was cracked, but it appeared to have been well cared for, if not loved. She looked up and said, "No. No, I'm not interested in Claudia. Now please tell me why you're asking."

"Because you can tell a lot about a person by how she treats her friends. Pity poor Harper Jenkins, is all I can say."

Confounded, Annie asked, "Why? What was Claudia saying about Harper?"

After an eye-popping, infuriating recounting of a conversation Laney had overheard – of Claudia's scathing assessment of Harper's unfortunate circumstance – Laney said, "You like her. Harper, I mean."

"Yes, I like her. She doesn't deserve for those things to be said about her. Especially not by a friend."

Laney came close and took Annie's hand. "Then go find her. Life is short, Annie. You know that better than anyone. And if you want to, offer her the study. A bed will fit in there. I'll move my office to my room."

Annie had always been grateful for her best friend, but in that moment, she had never been prouder of Laney Bates and her huge, generous heart. "I wish Claudia was to Harper what you are to me."

"Sometimes it takes rough sailing to show up the leaks. Seems to me Harper is taking on water because of that woman. Her hull could use some bracing, so go on. Go tell Harper she has a *real* friend."

* * *

Thursday, 23rd February, 2023

Claudia was driving home from work when the voice of news anchor, Justin Howell, came over the radio. As Claudia pulled into her street, she cranked the volume.

'Police are still investigating the disappearance of thirty-two-year-old waitress, Harper Jenkins, who was last seen five days ago at a surprise

birthday party that took place at a home in the coastal town of Penguin.
It's been established that she caught a ride to the party, but it seems she left
alone and hasn't been heard from since.

The alarm was raised by friends who also attended the celebration, and
they've told authorities they've been searching for Jenkins ever since she left
the gathering, which they estimate at around 9:30 p.m. Witnesses say she
was wearing black jeans and a white shirt, and carrying a blue handbag.
Anyone who has information on Harper Jenkins is encouraged to call Crime
Stoppers on-'

Claudia killed the radio. Every power pole she passed featured a
poster of Harper's smiling face, and above it, MISSING. Claudia pulled
up at the house, and moments later in the rearview mirror, spied a man
and a woman – both donning dark suits and sober expressions – loping
up the driveway. She'd known it would only be a matter of time before
they circled back to her.

Claudia checked her reflection in the rearview. Sweat had popped on
her brow, and her bottom lip was trembling. She gripped the wheel,
desperate for a way to explain. But how would she explain that it was
Annie and Laney – not Claudia – who had stuck hundreds of posters
across town in a bid to find their friend? How would she explain that
at the party and in a drunken state, she had watched Harper and Annie
together and become jealous to the point of seething? How would she
explain that on seeing Harper leave the party, she had gotten into her
car and followed her friend up a side street? How could she ever make
anyone understand that in the argument that ensued, Harper was
being unreasonable to the point of hysteria? How could she explain that
Harper's fall was an accident, that her cracked skull was never planned,
and that she might've tripped even if Claudia hadn't pushed her? And
how would she ever make anyone believe that throwing Harper in the
dumpster at the back of the bottle shop, that returning to the party in
a state of calm, was not an act of cowardice or of malice, but of survival?

The bearded fellow in the suit knocked on the driver's window.
"Claudia Lyle, I'm Detective Boyd. Please step out of the vehicle, ma'am."

The news report said nothing about a body.

Claudia wiped her wet brow.

They don't know it was you.

She combed her fingers through her gentle curls.

You don't belong in prison.

She reached down and unclasped her seatbelt.

You can do this.

Then she opened the door.

7

Write a story about someone seeking revenge for a past wrong.

LADY'S LAST OPERA

N oun: nemesis
(pl. nemeses)
1. Something causing misery or death
the nemesis of my life
= bane, curse, scourge

* * *

Connie Johns-Farrow woke up in the dark, with her cheek pressed against the silky breast of Summer Wilcox. Alone, sleeping in darkness was something Connie simply didn't do. Perhaps it was childish, but light reassured her. Since meeting Summer, the woman's embrace had evolved into a promise, and that was to keep Connie safe from whatever ill might be lurking in shadow. That was part of Summer's unspoken gift, and only the tip of the iceberg as far as Connie was concerned. The personal trainer was a firestorm of passion as well as an incurable romantic, but what Connie appreciated most about her was the trust Summer was able to elicit, which was for Connie a revelation.

Connie whispered, "Are you awake?"

Summer gave her a squeeze. "Very. Lady over the fence has been yapping an opera."

Connie chuckled. "The Barber of Seville?"

"More like Tosca."

"Ouch. I don't hear her now though."

"Maybe Gary fetched her inside. There's supposed to be a storm this morning."

Connie reached behind and switched on the bedside lamp. Then she positioned herself over the woman with the long dark mane, and hazel eyes that Connie wasn't sure she'd ever seen so intense.

Connie had a confession to make, but for now – for those eyes – she had to ask, "What are you thinking?"

Summer stroked Connie's naked shoulder. "You first."

Connie had no idea how Summer would react to what need be said. Some ground rules had been laid from the very beginning, and Connie was about to break them. She palmed the ivory palette of Summer's chest, then dropped a kiss on her heart-shaped lips. Summer's reply was tender and – Connie hoped – loving.

Connie said, "Last night was wonderful. All of it."

"You weren't disappointed?"

"Because we missed the show? No. You more than made up for that. In fact, it turned out so well," Connie tweaked an eyebrow, "I'm wondering if you didn't plan the whole thing."

"You give me too much credit. My plans never turn out that well." Summer's smile was half-hearted, and Connie wondered if that was her fault for not coming clean sooner.

"I need to be honest with you about something."

Still stroking Connie's shoulder, Summer replied simply, "Okay."

"I... I don't think I can honour our agreement."

The flicker that taunted Summer's brow, the ghost that inhabited her eyes, for all of the incumbent enigma, conveyed at minimum, discomfort. She brushed Connie's burnt-umber wisps behind her ear. "I'm not the one for you, Con."

Connie took a moment to bear witness, to contemplate Summer's categorical lack of conviction. "I don't believe you mean that."

"Understand that if I'd known how I was going to feel about you, I would never have..."

"Would never have what? Summer, please tell me."

The answer caught in Summer's throat, like a dirty big rat in a downpipe.

Connie frightened Summer with her hopeful eyes, yet more so with her unfettered affection. "I know you're keeping something from me; from the world. And I know we agreed we weren't going to get serious, but..."

Summer's own desire was long out of her control. Instead of shutting Connie down as she should, she prompted, "But what, C.J?"

"*But*... you are everything I've ever wanted, Summer Wilcox. This is everything I want, right here."

"Don't... don't say that."

"It's the truth. And I know that for whatever reason it makes you uncomfortable, but I also know you care about me."

Yes, Summer cared. But it wasn't part of the plan. And she couldn't abandon the plan.

Summer asked, "What do you know about the Greek goddess, Nemesis?"

"Summer, sweetheart, that is a terrible segue."

Summer rolled Connie over so that Summer herself was on top. "Come on. What do you know?"

Connie curled her fingers around the nape of Summer's neck. "Ah, okay. Well, I know Narcissus met his *end* thanks to her."

"So he did. The mountain nymph, Echo, had been robbed of a unique voice by Hera, for her part in enabling Zeus to carry out his affairs. One day in the woods, Echo caught sight of Narcissus and fell in love with him. But because she was doomed to only repeat the words of others, she couldn't tell him how she felt. He in turn cruelly spurned her, as he had so many others. On hearing the story, Nemesis decided some intervention was required, so she had Narcissus fall in love with his own reflection."

"In a pool of water."

"And there he died. Withered away, unable to take his eyes off himself, unable to satisfy his *lust*."

"Divine retribution?"

"Divine retribution. Most people, when they hear the word *nemesis*, think of an arch enemy, an indomitable opponent. But Nemesis to me is *retributive justice*."

Connie's interest turned to concern. "Did someone hurt you, Summer? Is that... is that why you need to keep me at arm's length? Because I would never hurt you. I would never."

Summer considered the sincerity ever present in those sombre green eyes. "I know that, Con." Summer at least *felt* she knew, but it didn't matter. *Dammit*, it wasn't part of the plan. She climbed off the docile woman and fixed the covers over her.

"Summer..."

Summer wandered to the chest of drawers opposite the foot of the bed. She opened the top drawer (which Connie had made available to her only days before), removed a nightshirt and slipped into it. Then she took up the Beretta 3032 Tomcat – a pocket pistol she'd purchased on the black market – and slid the magazine into the well. Having stopped short of racking the slide, Summer turned.

She didn't have the heart to point the thing, but she didn't need to. Even under the dim glow of the bedside lamp, Summer sensed Connie's almond complexion turn white.

Connie stammered, "What... what are you..."

"I'm sorry, Con. I didn't want this. I have been incredibly patient, but now... I need to know where he is."

"Where *who* is?"

"You *know* who. Lucas Farrow."

Connie drew the covers over her breasts. "Why? What do you want with him?"

"I've gone to considerable effort to find him. I realise now, he's not Lucas Farrow anymore, is he? He's hiding like the coward he is." Connie threw the comforter aside. Alarmed, Summer raised the pistol.

Connie climbed off the mattress and stood by the bed. Naked and vulnerable, she mumbled, "Considerable effort. *I* see." She bent over and retrieved her shirt, which had been discarded several hours prior in a fit of passion. "Do you mind?" she asked, rather redundantly as she slipped the apricot garment over her shapely frame without Summer's consent. Then she scooped her long mane from underneath the collar, and her soft curls bounced off her shoulders. She was doing her best to appear unaffected, and Summer might've been convinced except for the tear that rushed her colourless cheek. "Bravo, Summer. I had no idea."

"I didn't want this, Connie. Believe me. But I do *need* this. Tell me how to find your brother."

"*Step*brother." Connie took a step towards her.

Summer warned, "Don't." Connie stalled. Then she took another step. "Connie, stop!" But Connie didn't stop. She kept coming, forcing Summer to steady the small weapon with a second hand. Summer whispered, "Connie, *please*."

With the barrel only inches from her chest, Connie said, "This is about Mandy Knight. This is about the accident."

"There was no *accident*, Connie. Lucas *murdered* her."

Connie's brow formed an uncharacteristic line in its middle. "No. No, that *can't* be true. The police investigated. They cleared him of any wrongdoing."

"They didn't *clear* him of wrongdoing, Con. They just didn't make their case."

"Which was what, exactly?"

"It doesn't matter now. The law won't fix it."

"But Nemesis *can*?"

Summer stated, "Retributive *justice*."

"And so you spied on me."

Summer replied with an uncomfortable, "Yes."

"You... you schemed your way into my life hoping you could get closer to him."

"He was ob*sessed* with her! She told him no, but he wouldn't *listen*.

She was afraid of him, but he was careful. He knew *exactly* what he could get away with. But he's not going to get away with it. He's going to pay for what he did."

"And then what, Summer?"

"Then... then I'll pay for what *I've* done."

Connie muttered as though the walls had ears, "Even if it means going to jail for the better part of your *life*?"

"If the courts had put him away, I'd have been content with that. But they let him walk! As though her life meant *nothing!*" Whatever displeasure had knotted Connie's brow, in that moment melted away. Summer reigned in her anger. "Mandy Knight was like a sister to me. I won't let her killer go unpunished. I... I'm willing to accept the consequences of that."

"Well, it's nice to know you haven't considered me even *once* in all of your conniving."

Summer lowered the weapon. "I think you know that's not true."

"Then why didn't you just *ask* me?"

"I *have* asked you, C.J."

"Not with any kind of transparency, you haven't. And I've regardless answered honestly. I don't know where Lucas is." Summer felt thoroughly despicable under Connie's prickly gaze. Connie said, "The day we met: it was no accident you were handing flyers out at the café, was it?" Guilt further arrested Summer's tongue. Connie folded her arms. "You said I had an amazing suprasternal notch."

The memory was a fond one, prompting Summer's rueful smile. "You do have an amazing suprasternal notch."

"I had no idea what you were talking about."

"You said it must be from all the jumping jacks you did."

"I had no idea, but I was charmed anyway. How stupid I was."

"Connie, please—"

"You used me, Summer. And I get it. Lucas is a terrible person. You don't need to point a gun at me to convince me of that. You want justice for your friend, so please, let's not pretend this was anything other than convenient for you."

Summer ejected the magazine from the gun. She popped the Beretta's unique tip-up barrel and checked it was empty, then threw both items on the bed. She grasped Connie's hands and confessed, "It's true that at first, I got close to you because of him. But I never intended for us to..." Summer wiped the wet from Connie's cheek. "Then we shared a bed, and I learned more about you than I ever imagined. I don't know if you know this, but you talk in your sleep." Connie's lids draped, shifting more tears and providing a shield for her damaged soul. Summer revealed gently, "I know why you sleep with the light on. I know what he did to you, and trust me when I tell you, I am every bit as committed to making him pay for that as for what he did to Mandy." Connie lifted her eyes. Inside of them swirled a mixture of old pain and grudging gratitude. Summer said, "I know I told you that I didn't want us to get serious, but the truth is, I was already crazy as hell about you. I just... I knew that if things went to plan..."

Summer was interrupted by Connie's fingers on her jaw, was silenced by Connie's mouth on her lips, was roused by Connie's tongue on her tongue. Summer's responses were measured, not for lack of desire but for an awareness of the wrong she'd done. Still, Connie's affections surged. Her kisses were wild, her hands busy; smoothing over Summer's satin-shrouded flanks, down to her hips and over her buttocks. Summer's relief for Connie's apparent forgiveness released a passion that up until that moment had been curbed by guilt. Summer returned Connie's fire by rending them both naked and backing Connie to the bed. Connie lay down and Summer climbed on top, with every intention of making up her transgression.

After a ravenous kiss, Connie professed, "I'll go to the police. I'll tell them everything. They'll have no choice but to look for him."

What Connie was offering was immense. Within her family she would almost certainly be doubted, undoubtedly debated. She'd be thoroughly scrutinised, and scrutinously criticised. She might even be ostracised.

Summer's admiration for the woman peaked. "Are you sure? What about your mum?"

Connie cupped Summer's face in her hands. "I can handle it. But only if you're with me. Promise you'll be there with me. You have to promise me that."

Summer's reply could not have been more sincere. "You have my word, C.J."

Summer slid a hand over Connie's, and their fingers laced. Summer kissed her palm, and looked unflinchingly into her eyes.

Connie whispered, "Not part of the plan, I know, but I love you, Summer Wilcox."

Exhilarated, Summer donned a grin. "Then you won't mind what I'm about to do to you."

"As long as it's hot, sweaty, fantastic sex, I won't mind a bit."

Summer chuckled. "Well, how about that: I *am* the one for you, after all." Summer proceeded to fulfil Connie's wish, bringing her to a loud, shuddering climax that dispelled any notion of the pistol dropped on the floor, any care of the location of one Lucas Farrow.

* * *

He was dressed in black from top to toe – practically invisible – on this moonless, starless night. There was a palpable charge in the air. It might have been that a storm was brewing, but he also couldn't deny the thrill in his bones of finding the curtains to the boudoir part way open. Not *deliberately* open, *carelessly* open. Enough to enjoy the view of the bed, in any case.

Lucas Farrow waited for the incessant chatter to stop.

(*'There was no accident, Connie.'*)

Then he waited for the bullshit bravado to stop.

(*'I'll go to the police. I'll tell them everything.'*)

Then he waited for the endless *fucking* to stop.

(He might've put a stop to that himself, except that his cock got hard. He didn't see the harm in giving it a tug.)

Then he waited for the light to go out.

A flash from the heavens lit the darkened window, and in it he caught a glimpse of himself. Thunder rumbled. Within moments a lightning storm unleashed, turning the sky violet. The dazzling show gave Lucas a more sustained visage. He leaned close to the glass and turned his cheek. *Hello, handsome.* Chris Hemsworth, without the beady eyes. He wiped at a dark spot on his temple: gore from that pesky dog. Jack Russell? Scottish Terrier? Whatever its breed, it'd been too damned yappy for its own good.

Lucas took from his hip pocket the key: a treasure he'd stolen from his stepmother at a party in honour of his father (a gathering noticeably absent his stepsister). It was the first time he'd made contact with his old man in months, and it was there that he'd learned of Connie's new *friend*, Summer Wilcox.

No accident, indeed. He'd recognised the name. He knew *exactly* who she was.

Wilcox was right about one thing. The police did let him walk. And why not? Mandy Knight was trash. Lucas was simply providing a cleaning service. He'd get away with this, too. But the authorities wouldn't need to let him walk. They'd never even suspect he was here. The storm was providing the perfect cover, there would be no sign of forced entry, and the only prints on the gun would belong to Wilcox. A tragic murder/suicide.

Lucas Farrow sauntered to the back door, inserted the key, and slipped inside.

He hadn't fathomed that his self-appreciation in the window

might've alerted the occupants to his presence. He hadn't anticipated he'd be caught like a dormouse in a blinding beam of light. And he certainly hadn't expected the warm gush in his pants for the sound of a gun cocking.

"Hello, Narcissus," said that bitch, Summer Wilcox. "Nemesis has been waiting for you."

Epilogue

My therapist told me it would be helpful to write some shit down, so here it is! Gary's first day of journalling. Welcome!

It's a sunny day out, and my small companion has apparently decided to once again wander on over to the neighbours. It's been three months since Lady's operation. She's fully recovered from the brutal attack she suffered the night of that crazy storm, but the vet wasn't able to save her leg. She's adjusted quickly though, and gets around just super.

The lovely couple next door spoil her rotten. C.J. and Summer could not have been more caring when they found out what had happened to Lady that night, and they've doted on her ever since. Their place has become Lady's second home. The strangest thing though: there is a patch of ground in their back yard that seems to give her the *angries*. She barks and then relieves herself over it every time she visits. I've apologised to them profusely, but they don't seem to mind a bit. Two very cool ladies.

I still don't know who attacked my fur baby that night. I admit, the thought of the sick bastard getting away with it was making me ill, but Connie told me something recently that gave me some comfort.

'Nemesis is an old soul, Gary. She doesn't care for the tired excuses of bad men. She only cares about justice. I trust her. Like no one else, I trust her. You should too.'

I don't know why, but I believed her.

8

*Set your story in a rosy-pink world where everything
is rainbows and unicorns… until it isn't.*

THE DIMMING
OF THE LIGHT

I t was the strangest thing. All the globes in the house had blown, all at the same time.

Lexi Banks stood before the bathroom mirror. Her reflection reminded her of a zombie spawned from one of those gruesome video games. Her ghastly appearance may have been due to the low wattage of one of the only spare globes she could find, but it seemed more likely she'd aged a lifetime overnight. The shadows under her eyes, the onyx of her dim bulbs, the black trenches that ran across her brow and under her bottom lip. It might not have been her reflection at all, but rather a vision of her corpse.

The silken sleeve of her nightgown slid to her elbow as she opened the cabinet. Inside were two kinds of pills: one a ginger concoction marketed to pregnant women who weren't enjoying their bouts of morning sickness, the other a sleeping aid. It was too dark in there to tell which was which, and though she was suffering from both nausea and insomnia, Lexi decided against both. She closed the cabinet, then smoothed her hands over her belly. "We love you, kiddo. We both love you... *so* much."

Lexi shuffled to the bed, slid under the covers, and cried herself to sleep.

* * *

"Hey, lovely lady."

Lexi opened sleepy eyes. Through the dark, red numerals announced the time: 01:02. A warm body was pressed against her back, and an arm was slung around her waist. The familiar scent of peony and jasmine brought a smile.

Without lifting her head from the pillow, she said, "You're home already?"

"I was about to board when I got the message the meeting had been cancelled." Tyler's warm breath tickled her lobe. "Did you miss me?"

"In four hours? I barely noticed you were gone."

"You lie." Tyler pecked her temple. "Are you still mad?"

Lexi considered further teasing, but her heart wasn't in it. The truth was, she felt awful for the way they had left things. She switched on the bedside lamp and rolled over. Facing her was a thirty-two-year-old brunette, whose recent shorter cut was just as becoming as any previous length she'd donned. Her light brown eyes carried a guilt that Lexi wanted to dispel.

"I'm not mad, Tee."

"You know I would never have left if it wasn't important."

Lexi nodded. She'd known it from the moment Tyler had mentioned the impromptu trip, but she'd overreacted nonetheless. "I got a little crazy. I'm sorry."

Tyler touched light fingers to Lexi's jaw. "It's okay. I should've been more sensitive."

"It wasn't your fault. I just… I'm sure it's the hormones, but I had this overwhelming dread that something bad was going to happen."

"What do you mean? What kind of *bad*?" When Lexi didn't answer, Tyler probed. "Lexi, darling, please tell me. Are you alright? Is it the baby?"

"We're fine." Lexi whispered, "*We* are fine."

Tyler gave her the side-eye. "Ah. This is about the flight."

Yes. "No."

"Yes."

"No."

"Yesss." Tyler chuckled. Lexi wished she thought it funny. Qantas was the safest airline in the world, but knowing that hadn't dispelled her sudden, atypical fear.

"Hey." Tyler snuggled close. "This was going to be my last trip away, okay? I'm here now. You are stuck with me, Lexi Banks. And I have a surprise for you."

"A surprise?"

Tyler jumped out of the bed, wearing white coveralls conspicuously splashed with pink. "Come on." She took Lexi's hand. "Come and see."

One minute later and with eyes closed, Lexi had been guided through the door of Baby's room. Tyler hugged her from behind and rested her hands on Lexi's swollen belly. "Okay," Tyler said. "You can open them now."

What Lexi opened her eyes to, was a dazzling display of colour. At the centre of a wall of hot pink, were two frolicking white unicorns with yellow horns. They were facing each other, cheek to cheek, both on back hooves sunken into splashes of green. Their rainbow tails were swept in an imaginary breeze that could only have belonged to spring, and Lexi could almost smell the cherry blossom.

"Oh, Tee. You finished it."

"What do you think?"

Lexi turned in Tyler's arms. She was so ill-practiced at verbalising her emotions, she wasn't sure she could convey adequately, those feelings that had only ever been inspired within her by this woman who held her so tight. Not that Tyler had seemed to mind. The disparate communication that Lexi had forced upon their relationship – the same reluctance of hers that had most assuredly driven others away – had solidified the pairing into one that had outshone any other, had brought Tyler so deeply into Lexi's heart that at first, she was terrified. How did people do this? How could it be considered sensible to allow someone such open access to the innermost sanctum of one's heart? It seemed to Lexi a kind of insanity, and so she had kept to a minimum her own use of those three little words, which, after all, must have formed the most overused expression of *any* language. She had never wanted to discourage Tyler with her outward dispassion, but at the same time was afraid of the vulnerability that Tyler had so manifestly and endlessly evoked. Not that Tyler had ever betrayed it.

While Lexi was grappling with her thoughts, Tyler said, "I can paint over it if you like."

There was a sadness in the offering that Lexi had not meant to invoke, and had not the heart to ignore. She planted a palm on Tyler's chest. "No, you won't, Tyler Devereaux."

Tyler replied with a wisp of a smile, "It's okay?"

"It's perfect."

Obviously pleased, Tyler slipped her hands over Lexi's hips. "I really wanted to do this for her. And you know, there are still three more walls begging for inspiration. Maybe the two of us could—"

Lexi blurted, "I love you."

Of *course*, Lexi loved her. She and Tyler had moved in together, had planned a family together, had planned a *life* together. Those words should not have been foreign, and Lexi in that moment felt a panic born of shame that she hadn't made herself more familiar with the lexical representation of her inner landscape, which without Tyler would have been barren.

Lexi repeated, "I love you, Tee."

"My darling Lex, I know that."

"I'm so sorry I haven't told you more often. I... I don't know why I haven't."

Tyler let her go. Then she folded her arms and tweaked an eyebrow. "Okay, what is it? Are you having an affair? It's the OBGYN, isn't it? Those titillating exercise machine commercials of her *flamboyant* youth. What was it now. Oh, Ab-Strict? Easy Buns? Bet she's loaded, too."

Tyler's mischievous grin did not alleviate Lexi's panic. "I feel... I feel like I've let you down."

"Lex, no. I promise, you haven't."

"I..." Tears rushed her cheeks. Air left her lungs.

Tyler gripped her shoulders. "Listen to me, Lex. Do you think I'd be here, do you think I'd be having a baby with you, if I didn't *know*?" She cradled Lexi's jaw with both hands. "No matter what happens, my darling, always remember: I *know*, and I love you." She placed a delicate kiss on Lexi's lips. Lexi returned it with passion.

Lexi's heart was pounding. But it wasn't the pleasant overarching beat of arousal. It was a sudden, maniacal tremor of terror. *Oh please, God, don't let it be too late.*

There was a popping sound, and the room went dark.

* * *

Lexi woke to her phone vibrating against the bedside dresser. One eye was buried in her pillow, the other she directed at the alarm clock. 10:06. Lexi never slept past eight.

She dragged herself upright and leaned against the headboard. Tyler's side of the bed was neat. The curtains were still closed.

"Tee?" Lexi threw the covers aside and climbed off the bed. "Tee?" Her limbs felt like lead, and when she stood, the room swayed like Aunt Jacki after a blinder.

Lexi slipped into her gown, palmed her phone and shuffled through the hallway to the kitchen. There was no coffee brewing, no note on the bench. The Samsung vibrated in her pocket. Lexi checked the screen. There were two missed calls from a number she didn't recognise, but more importantly, there was a missed call from Tyler. She was about to check the voice message when the doorbell rang. Feeling entirely unpresentable, Lexi considered not answering.

The doorbell rang again.

On the stoop was a young, uniformed police officer, who removed his crisp white hat and placed it under his armpit. "Ms Banks?"

"Yes."

"I'm Officer Kyle Lamprey of Knoxfield police."

"What... what is it I can do for you, Officer Lamprey?"

Officer Lamprey's Adam's Apple bobbed. "You're, um, you're listed as..."

Lexi's heart was pounding. She only ever remembered it pounding like this the once, and it had happened just that morning, in Baby's room right before the lights blew. She'd considered she might've been having a heart attack.

"Ms Banks?"

"I'm sorry, what... what did you say?"

"You're listed as Tyler Devereaux's next of kin?"

Yes. But why on earth should he be asking her that? Lexi studied the blue uniform, then looked over Lamprey's shoulder at the marked car with the mounted lights, parked at the curb.

She reluctantly nodded.

"Ms Banks," he said, "Tyler Devereaux was involved in a car accident just after 1 a.m. this morning. It seems she was enroute to her hotel, after landing at Sydney airport at around 12.30. Her taxi was hit by another taxi. Emergency responders arrived shortly after, and Ms Devereaux was transported to the Royal Prince Alfred hospital. Ms Banks, it's my sad duty to inform you that Ms Devereaux passed away from her injuries. An investigation is underway, and those officers will be in touch with you soon. Ms Banks, I am...I am so sorry for your loss."

* * *

Lexi hadn't argued with Lamprey. She'd simply thanked him and watched him leave. Clearly, there had been some horrendous mistake. A mistake of identity, or perhaps some galling administrative error. She felt terrible for the family who would at some point rightly receive the news, but it wasn't *Lexi's* family. It wasn't Lexi's news.

She took the phone from her pocket and checked on Tyler's call. The screen showed:

Thursday, 27 July 2023
15283548.amr
101 MessageBank

Tyler tapped play and pressed the phone to her ear.

'My darling Lexi. I guess you're sleeping. I just... I wanted to apologise for

us leaving things the way we did. This trip seemed so damned important, but now that I'm here, I wish I'd stayed home. I wished I'd just... crawled into bed with you. I know I've told you this before, but you and Baby have made me so incredibly happy.'

A man's voice said, *'Looks like we need to make a detour, Miss.'*

'Oh, okay. Lex, I'm almost at the hotel, so I gotta go. I'll call in a few hours. And I'll be home as soon as I can. And then I'm going to make it up to you, starting with a pair of unicorns. Lexi, darling, I love—"

An explosive din – a ruckus that made no sense – abruptly ended the message. Stunned, Lexi checked the time of the call: 1:01am.

* * *

What are you waiting for?
You know she was here. She was here.

Walking into that room was the hardest thing Lexi had ever done. She did it with her eyes shut, and once inside, pressed her back firmly against the door.

She could feel Tyler's arms around her, could smell her perfume.

Oh please, God, don't let it be too late...

Lexi opened her eyes.

In the first, paint tins lined against the wall.

A pile of drop-sheets, clean and neatly folded.

Paint trays and rollers, and a collection of brushes with pristine bristles still sheathed in their clear plastic sleeves.

A neatly folded pair of white coveralls.

There was no hot pink, only a lifeless pale yellow. One wall displayed a pencil outline of two equine beasts, each with a long thin triangle protruding from a bold forehead.

On unsteady feet she approached. Then with a shaky finger, Lexi caressed the familiar grey outline, from noble crown to sturdy hoof. She noticed beneath one of them, a discretely scribed dedication: *For our daughter. LB+TD.*

* * *

It was the strangest thing. All the globes in the house had blown, all at the same time.

Lexi shuffled to the bed, slid under the covers, and cried herself to sleep.

9

Write a story about someone trying to resist their darker impulses.

TAMING THE FLAME

F arrah fixed her sleeveless summer dress, then headed from the bathroom through the hallway towards the chattering of guests. As she approached the living room where the congregation was gathered, she noticed her study door was open when it shouldn't have been. Indeed, it *hadn't* been when she'd passed it only minutes earlier. She popped her head in, and was unnerved that her laptop was open and the screen lit.

Farrah wandered to the desk. The Word document displayed was an untitled message; an attack in the guise of 'wisdom'.

Dear Farrah,

I'm telling you this as a friend. I know it will be hard for you to hear, but that doesn't make the message any less true.

This little book of yours is never going to garner the attention you imagine it deserves. It's not going to launch you into stardom, or a career. If not for the fleshless quality of the ebook, Taming the Flame would gather dust on shelves in lofts, be eaten by silverfish in boxes in basements. No one is going to care about your hollow characters or their tired exploits. They won't care for your spiritless prose.

These words are for you only. Publicly, I will only ever support you, will wholeheartedly praise you. I'm not a monster, after all. I just wish I could spare you the inevitable disappointment that is incumbent upon this venture.

I do hope you'll accept this not as subjective detriment, but as objective wisdom.

- M

* * *

Jackie was in the kitchen, helping her daughter by preparing another platter of meats and cheeses, when Lana DeGroot wandered in from the busy living room. Jackie guessed that Lana was around her age, with similar soft grey curls and roughly the same crow's feet scratching about the eyes. Although, Lana's spectacles were somewhat more garish.

Smiling, Lana stepped to the counter. "It's wonderful that you came today, Jackie."

"Well, of course. It's a big day for my girl."

"Debut novel. You must be very proud."

"I am. Very much so."

"Have you read the book yet?"

"Well of course I have, Lana. And I can tell you this. Farrah got her talent from her mother. Her father didn't know a verb from a vacuum cleaner." Both women chuckled.

Lana said, "Do you want me to bus this platter for you? It's like there's a bunch of locusts out there this afternoon."

"Thank you, Lana. That would be much appreciated." With a wink, Lana took up the loaded dish and exited through the kitchen's double doors.

Farrah sprang from the hallway and rushed over to close those same doors. Then she stood across the counter from Jackie with a grim look on her young face. "Mum, has anyone been through here in the last few minutes?"

"What do you mean?"

"When I went through to the bathroom, did... did someone follow me?"

"To the *bathroom*?"

"Did someone come through not long after?"

"Oh." Jackie opened a box of crackers. "Molly. Just a few minutes ago."

Farrah's expressive blue eyes reflected a sudden, untold hurt. "*Molly*? Mum, are you sure?"

"I'm not senile just yet, dear."

"There... there must've been someone else."

"No, darling. Just Molly." Jackie retrieved the vintage cheddar from the fridge, then returned to the counter and placed the cheese on the chopping board.

Farrah's expression was still taut when she said, "You didn't have to do this, Mum."

"Well of course I did. That's what mums do. Now go enjoy your party with all of your wonderful friends."

* * *

It was a fine day out, and the north-facing floor-to-ceiling windows allowed inside every glorious ray. The glass doors were open, and guests moved freely between the inner sanctum and the balcony. Farrah should've been rapt that folks were discussing her book with such enthusiasm, but the note – and the thought that Molly had left it – well and truly soured the moment.

Farrah spied Molly outside, leaned against the railing with a wine glass in hand. She'd been the first to show, had helped Farrah with the last-minute preparations. She'd even bought Farrah a gift; as yet unopened, but a gesture nonetheless sweet and very much appreciated.

Farrah adored Molly. Not that she'd ever openly said so. Farrah was impossibly shy when it came to such feelings; especially when they involved women. Today Molly wore a crisp white shirt with the sleeves rolled, tapered black pants, and heeled sandals. Her kind green eyes were hidden behind a pair of sunglasses, and her mahogany hair wisped delicately about her face. Her red lips were parted in a generous smile.

She was chatting with a tall, dark-headed fellow named George, and Farrah slipped out onto the deck so that she might eavesdrop on the conversation.

George asked, "Have you known Farrah long?"

"Almost a year. We met at a writer's workshop."

"Oh, you're a writer too?"

"Short stories mostly. I'm happy for anything that can fit into a DL envelope. I hope to be as good as Farrah one day. I honestly can't imagine having the staying power for a novel."

"Isn't a novel just a bunch of short stories tied together?"

"Ah, how I wish it were so, George. Think of it this way. A novel is a marriage. A series of short stories is a bunch of one-night stands. The latter might always keep you active, but you wouldn't call the sum total of all that *bedhopping* a relationship."

George declared, "Ah! Monogamy!"

"Right? Long term exclusivity." They laughed together.

George said, "Well, maybe you can pick up a few pointers from the lovely Farrah."

Molly looked down at the glass in her hands. Then she looked up again and replied, "I'd like that. Very much."

George held up his tumbler, then excused himself and wandered away. Molly rested her forearms on the railing and looked out over the wide ocean vista.

Farrah quietly approached and stood beside her.

Molly turned and beamed. "Well, there you are, Miss Newly Published."

Farrah replied flatly, "Here I am."

Molly's pleasure dimmed. She touched Farrah's elbow. "Hey, is something wrong?" When Farrah's only answer was a trembling lower lip, Molly removed her shades. She peered over Farrah's shoulder, then stepped closer and murmured, "Far, what is it?" Farrah handed Molly a print-out. Molly unfolded the A4 slip and proceeded to scan. Then she looked up with a clustered brow. "Who wrote this?"

"*Em*. 'M' wrote it, Molly."

"Well, who is..." What Farrah's previous tone had lacked, evidently her dour expression made up. Molly breathed, "You think this was *me*?" Regardless of, or perhaps due to, Farrah's reticence, disbelief manifested in Molly's emerald depths. She cloaked it with her dark glasses, but even through those gloomy lenses Farah sensed displeasure. When Molly proceeded to walk away, Farrah grabbed her arm.

She whispered, "I found it on my computer. Whoever wrote this is here *right* now."

"And because someone signed off with an *M*, you think it was me?"

"I don't *want* to think it, Molly."

"Then why are you thinking it? Just stop, okay? Stop thinking it."

Before Farrah could utter another word, Molly took her by the hand and led her through the swarm of guests from the balcony to the living room, past (a baffled) Jackie in the kitchen, to the study. She closed the door behind them, then took off her glasses and turned on Farrah her determination. "Show me."

"Why?"

"Show me." Not sure what difference it would make, Farrah went to the desk and pawed at the laptop. The document appeared. Molly bent at the hips and squinted at the screen. Then she stood tall and declared, "Sans Serif."

"What?"

"The font. Sans Serif. You write in Sitka."

Farrah checked the font bar. Molly was right. Farrah's Word program was automatically set to start every document in Sitka. Someone had changed it.

Molly ambled closer with soft eyes. "What's my font, Far?"

Farrah winced for embarrassment. "It's... it's Garamond. It's always Garamond."

Molly reached low for Farrah's hand. "None of what's in this letter is true. Sake, woman, I'm your biggest fan. Don't you know that? Far, tell me you know that." There was something in her voice and in those eyes; something other than sincerity. Farrah recognised it as lust, and suddenly her heart was pumping inordinate amounts of overheated blood through her veins. And then Molly's face was in Farrah's hands. And Molly's hands were on Farrah's hips. And then Farrah's lips were on Molly's mouth, and Molly's hands were caressing Farrah's butt. Farrah slid her fingers under the hem of Molly's shirt, felt the silky skin of her flanks and the erotic dip of her lumbar. Molly's tongue met Farrah's, and the thought of that fleshy organ on other parts of her fed Farrah's rapidly escalating desire.

* * *

70 minutes earlier...

Jackie rang the bell of the double storey brown brick home, for the first time ever.

Moments later the door opened.

Farrah's painted pink lips formed an O. "*Mum.*"

"Hello, my darling."

"I... I didn't know you were coming."

"I do hope it's okay. Aunt Kathy told me about your wonderful achievement. I thought I'd stop by and offer my congratulations."

"Th... thank you. Of course it's okay. Come in."

Jackie entered the foyer, and was faced by a woman she didn't recognise.

Farrah stood next to the stranger and said, "Mum, this is my good and charming friend, Molly."

The brunette stabbed a hand at her. "Mrs Day, it's so nice to finally meet you. Although I should warn you, Farrah exaggerates my abilities of the *good* and the *charming.*"

"I trust her judgment. It's wonderful to finally meet one of Farrah's friends." Jackie noticed a small parcel in Farrah's grip. "Oh, is that a gift?"

Farrah smiled at her acquaintance.

Molly slid open the drawer of the entry table and suggested to Farrah, "Why don't you open it later?" Farrah seemed happy with that, and placed the gift inside.

Then Farrah said, "Come upstairs, Mum. I'll pour you a glass of wine."

* * *

While Farrah greeted new arrivals, Molly entertained Jackie in the living room. They sat in a generously sized beige suede lounge, and on the wall, Jackie was confronted with a poster-sized print of the cover of Farrah's book, *Taming the Flame*. It was so large and the cover so orange, Jackie imagined the entire wall engulfed by fire. Underneath was a short table stacked with copies of the tome.

"So," said Molly, "you must be very proud of Farrah. She's a wonderful writer. I *am* her friend, but I'm also her biggest fan." Jackie brought the glass of red to her mouth. Molly asked, "Have you read the book, Mrs Day?"

Jackie replied brightly, "Well of course I have, Molly, and I can tell you this. Farrah got her talent from her mother. Her father didn't know a verb from a vacuum cleaner." Jackie chuckled.

Molly squinted. "Farrah's *dead* father, you mean?"

Jackie fidgeted in her lap. "Oh, Molly. Of course, I meant no disrespect."

"Of course you didn't. I mean, at least he was here for her, right?" Molly condemned her with a scowl.

"Molly, I don't know what you've been told—"

Molly checked over her shoulder, then murmured a menace. "Well, it's all there isn't it? In Farrah's book? Chapter nine is particularly enlightening. I know all there is to know about you, Jackie. I'm not sure why you're here today, but if you upset Farrah in any way, I *will* remove you."

"Why would I—"

"Don't underestimate me, Jackie. I know where you live."

Jackie was gobsmacked to the point of silence. A bunch of new guests arrived, and Molly stood and greeted them with what Jackie now recognised as façade.

* * *

A short while later, Jackie was in the kitchen alone, when Molly dragged Farrah from the living room, past Jackie into the hallway. Jackie rushed to the mouth of the corridor, and watched the two women disappear into the study. After checking over her shoulder, Jackie padded after them. The door was closed, and she pressed her ear to it.

"None of what's in this letter is true. Sake, woman, I'm your biggest fan. Don't you know that? Far, tell me you know that."

It grew quiet then. No shouting. No arguing. A light thump against the door made Jackie flinch. The sounds that followed were muffled, but once the heavy breathing started, Jackie required not much imagination to guess the goings on.

Farrah clearly had no idea what she was getting into. Molly was duplicitous. She was malicious. She might even be deranged; a predator who had obviously pulled the wool over Farrah's eyes. That they were obviously more than friends only made it worse. Wasn't it Jackie's job as a mother to protect her child from *exactly* these kinds of threats?

Lustful moans only fuelled her distress. Who was this woman to question Jackie's parenting? Jackie was a *good* mother. She didn't appreciate being accused – *vilified* – by a total stranger. She also didn't appreciate the thought that Molly might drive a wedge between Jackie and her only child.

She recalled the meeting in the foyer; how Molly had seemed so amenable. Every good predator knew the art of camouflage. Presenting gifts, for example, to win over – to *charm* – their target. Oh yes, the *good and charming* Molly.

Jackie wasn't in any state to deal with this now. She would leave, and serve Farrah some much needed advice, only when the girl was on her own and out of Molly's reach.

In the downstairs foyer, Jackie scanned for her heels among the many pairs of shoes that now dwelled inside the doorway. She checked over her shoulder into the empty stairwell, then drifted to the entry table and opened the drawer. Inside was Molly's gift to Farrah, the contents of which was none of Jackie's business. She tore into the wrapper. Inside was a red velvet box with a hinged lid, and inside of *that*, was an admittedly stunning necklace: a silver chain carrying a tear-shaped 'fire opal'. True to its name, the colour of the gem was a vivacious blood-orange blaze. A tiny scroll was also inside, which Jackie carefully unrolled.

For Farrah,
The Tamer of the Flame.
Love always,
The flame.

Jackie pocketed the gift; clearly just another weapon in Molly's arsenal of seduction, and without question Jackie's duty to remove. Would Farrah be angry with her for it? Surely not when she understood Jackie had no choice.

She had no choice.

In the drawer was another package: a flat rectangular box with the Zippo trademark printed at the top. She lifted the lid. Stored neatly within was a scarred metal lighter, a half-full wheel of flints, and a can of lighter fluid.

Was Farrah a smoker? Jackie would've known the answer had Farrah not been so distant; so *dismissive*.

Had the note Jackie left on Farrah's computer failed to cause a rift? Apparently, Farrah was more naïve than even Jackie had suspected.

Was Farrah right now copulating with someone dangerous? It seemed clear she was.

Was it Jackie's job to intervene? Well, who *else* was going to do it, if not the mother?

Jackie decided it was not quite time to leave, after all.

She took the cannister from the drawer.

* * *

Investigative notes, Officer Del U. Shone.

Fire/Arson at 12 Hingston Court.

Suspect: Jackie Day.

Victim: Farrah Day (Suspect's daughter).

Emergency services responded to a report of fire, and arrived at 16:10 to a burning two storey residential building.

Witness statements confirm preliminary findings that the fire started in the living room. A table of books was doused with lighter fluid and set alight. A fire extinguisher had earlier been removed, which hampered efforts of witnesses to douse the fire. Much of the upper level was affected before emergency services arrived. The home extinguisher was later found in the back yard, having evidently been tossed off the balcony. Fingerprint analysis confirmed the suspect had handled the device.

The suspect's statements to investigating officers have been difficult to verify. She claims to have spoken to a middle-aged woman named Lana DeGroot. No such person has been identified as attending the party, nor is known to Farrah Day or any of the guests.

The suspect claims that prior to the fire, she was engaged in a conversation with Molly Greene, and that during this conversation Ms Greene threatened her. She also claims they were interrupted by the arrival of new guests. Ms Greene vehemently denies the conversation happened. She asserts her attempts to engage with the suspect were met with hostility. Witnesses confirm Ms Greene's assertion that the suspect was alone on the balcony when they arrived, and that Ms Greene was preparing food platters alone in the kitchen.

Witnesses describe the suspect's demeanour as distant, uncommunicative and 'cold'.

The suspect seemed to have taken a dislike to Ms Greene, which became apparent upon interview.

Some minor smoke inhalation was suffered by guests trying to subdue the fire, but there were no serious casualties.

The suspect's motivation is unclear. After her initial claim that Ms Greene had started the fire (and after being presented with numerous witness reports that the suspect was herself responsible), she insists that she didn't *want* to start a fire, but that she felt compelled to do so. While she claims all of her actions were to help her daughter, she was unable to explain how lighting a fire in the victim's home would accomplish this.

The suspect is currently undergoing a psychiatric assessment, and pending the results of those enquires will likely be charged.

End notes.

10

*Set your story before dawn. Your character has
woken up early for a particular reason.*

SOLSTICE

J une 22nd, 1995
Part 1 – The Lie.

It was the morning of the winter solstice; the shortest day and the longest night, so that when the clock-radio flashed 4 a.m., it was still a long way from dawn.

Holly slapped her hand down over the bleating box, but it was too late. Lacey groaned to the tune of *You Oughta Know*, the bedside lamp came on, and Holly was greeted with Lacey's messy brown hair and squinting eyes.

Lacey moaned, "It can't be four already."

Holly squirmed under the covers till she was comfortably atop the sleepy lady. "Why did you even set the alarm? You're not the one catching the redeye, and you know I always wake up early."

Lacey draped her arms over Holly's shoulders. "I didn't want you sneaking away again."

"I never sneak. You always know when I'm leaving."

"Why does it always have to be so early? Just once I'd like to enjoy a lazy breakfast with you. Just once I'd like to be fully awake when you break my heart by walking out that door."

"Don't say that. You know I hate leaving you. There's just so much going on right now. You *know* I can't take my foot off the pedal. At least, not yet."

"I know. I just…" Lacey looked into Holly with those unashamedly affectionate eyes. It was a look that always warmed Holly's insides, but also reminded her of the lie. Lacey said, "I haven't asked. How's Mena doing?"

The last thing Holly wanted was to talk about her sister. "She's coping. Hey, do you know what today is?"

Lacey stroked Holly's hair. "What's today?"

"The winter solstice. One of the most spiritually significant days of the year. Do you know why?"

"Tell me."

Holly obliged with a voice that bypassed deception; that wrung straight from the most honest, sincerest, the most hopeful part of her. "It's the day when the dark is strongest, when it's at its zenith, when the light finds its nadir. But it's also a turning point. The darkness begins to cede, and the light starts upon its triumphant return."

Lacey caressed the nape of Holly's neck. She guided Holly to her with a gentle downward pressure, and they shared a slow, lingering kiss.

Lacey whispered, "Stay with me. Please."

Holly's heart ached. She didn't want to leave, and she hated having to keep up the charade. She felt trapped, and none of it was Lacey's fault. "You deserve better, Lace. Don't think I don't know that. I just... I need more time. If you can give me that, I promise things will get better."

Lacey's answer was another kiss – much livelier than the first – and although Holly was on a clock, she indulged the woman's much appreciated passion.

* * *

Three months earlier...

"Thanks for agreeing to meet with me, Miss Dunham. I'm so sorry I'm late."

"Call me Holly."

Lacey fumbled with the chair, catching the leg with her left toe. She sat, exasperated for what was proving to be a very rushed morning.

At the same moment the waitress arrived, Holly asked, "Are you alright?"

Lacey blustered, "Much needed double shot soy latte, please." The waitress imparted an unusually large grin before bustling away. Lacey turned her attention again to Holly, who combed a finger through her lustrous black hair. Lacey replied, "I'm well. Why do you ask?"

"Well, it's just... the top button of your shirt isn't matching the top hole."

Lacey looked down at her lopsided mauve blouse, and her cheeks burned; so hot, in fact, that in eight minutes they might've been worthy of a garnish of parsley and a side-serve of salad greens. "Oh, Jesus." Holly chuckled while Lacey righted herself, one button at a time.

Holly said, "Pardon the bold assumption, but I'm guessing you're not a morning person."

"I'm not, honestly. I tend to keep vampire hours."

"Ah. Well, I'm sorry I insisted on an early meeting, but I do have a killer schedule today."

"Oh, no, it's fine. Really. I'm grateful you squeezed me in."

The waitress dropped off the order just as Lacey extracted a notepad and pen from her handbag.

"So," said Holly, "where would you like to start?"

"Before we do, I just want to say I am so sorry for what's happening. How's your sister coping?"

"I appreciate that. And she's... as you'd expect, I guess. Messy, but hopeful."

"Well, I'm glad she's not given up. What about you? I imagine this is all very difficult for you as well."

Holly stared with her crystal green eyes, as though Lacey had said something profound. Or profoundly stupid. "I'm not particularly close to Mitch. But it's hard watching Mena suffer."

"They've been married three years?"

Holly nodded. "I guess you could say it was a fairy-tale romance. All princes and glass slippers and pumpkins turning into carriages." She swirled a dismissive hand through the air.

Lacey raised a brow. "Pardon *my* bold assumption, but something tells me you don't believe in fairy-tales."

Holly laughed and brought her cup to supple, unpainted lips. "On the record, Miss Koogan, I don't know what you mean."

As she sipped, Lacey noticed short glossy nails, and a white shirt cut in a way that flattered an ample bosom. There was also a mischief about the woman that Lacey found endearing.

Lacey asked, "And off the record, Miss Dunham?"

The black cup chinked against the saucer. Holly replied with playful enthusiasm, "Mitch Gordon is a cad. A jumpsuit made of iron couldn't keep that thing secured."

Lacey might've laughed if the man wasn't the subject of an ongoing search that began four days earlier. She asked quietly, "Are you suggesting he was unfaithful to your sister?"

"On the record, Miss Koogan?"

"Lacey. Please, call me Lacey."

"Lacey. On the record – and truthfully – Mena believes Mitch to be a faithful husband. Ultimately, I suppose, my opinion of him really doesn't matter."

There was a sadness about her then, that had Lacey wanting to dispense with the *record* entirely. "Your opinion matters to me. Your sister isn't talking to the press, and everyone else I've spoken to has suggested Mitch Gordon is beyond reproach. If you have a different opinion – on or off the record – I'm listening."

Holly leaned across and brought her hand gently down over Lacey's. Lacey's resting heartbeat kicked into high gear, not only for the woman's touch, but for her unwavering stare. It was the first time since her (adulterous) last partnership that she'd felt any kind of attraction. She'd not seen *that* trainwreck coming, had blithely disregarded her best friend's warnings of infidelity.

Holly murmured, "Mitch Gordon is a—"

The waitress returned, and Holly shot back in her seat.

"Is there anything else I can get for you ladies?"

Holly checked her watch. "Not for me, thanks."

Lacey echoed, "No, thank you." The waitress's departure allowed for more of Lacey's trademark mortification. "I really was late, wasn't I?"

"I really do have to go."

"Of course. I'm... I'm so sorry."

Holly stood and slung a handbag over her shoulder.

Lacey rose from her chair. "Maybe we could reschedule? I swear I won't keep you waiting a second time."

"Look, Lacey, I really don't know anything. He's my brother-in-law, yes, but I've had very little to do with him. I expect he'll be found on one of his bush trails somewhere, hunkering down because of a broken compass."

Lacey was discouraged by Holly's abrupt withdrawal. "I'm sure you're right. And we don't... we don't have to talk about him."

"Oh. Is there something else you wanted to discuss?"

Lacey stammered, "Well, no. Not... I mean, not... not specifically." *God, Lacey.*

Holly's initially blank expression convinced Lacey she'd again be chumming it up with her close pal, Humiliation. But then Holly's mouth formed a smile which was promptly dancing in her provocative eyes.

"Don't take this the wrong way, Lacey Koogan, but how long have you been working with the local rag?"

"A month if I'm not fired by Monday."

Holly rounded the table and came intimately close. Her proximity stirred butterflies, as did her hand on Lacey's forearm. "Tell you what. I'll talk to Mena, see if she'll agree to an interview with you. Before Monday. I'd hate to see you get fired."

Surprised, and yet more grateful, Lacey gushed, "You'd do that?"

"I would, on one condition."

Emboldened, Lacey replied suggestively, "Anything, Miss Dunham."

Holly grinned with rosy cheeks. "Well, I *was* going to suggest you be on time. But now that you've agreed to *anything...*"

* * *

22nd June, 1995
Part 2 – The Body.

Holly was in the shower, and Lacey was contemplating joining her when the clock-radio's snooze function kicked in. A news report came on, and Lacey was promptly sickened by it.

'The body of missing local man, Mitch Gordon, was discovered just after 1 a.m. this morning in a shack in the outskirts of Shepparton in northern Victoria. The cause of death is yet to be determined. Police believe that although Gordon has been missing since March, he's been dead less than twenty-four hours. Police are remaining tight-lipped as to whether Gordon was abducted or had disappeared of his own volition, but initial reports suggest he was being held at the property against his will. Forensics are on the scene, and police expect to have more answers in the coming days and weeks. Mitch Gordon is survived by his wife, Mena Gordon.'

Moments later, a muted jingle came from the handbag on the corner armchair. It occurred to Lacey in that moment that Holly never left her phone out: a quirk notorious of her ex. She jumped out of bed and rifled through Holly's things – makeup, keys, Qantas wallet – and found the Nokia with its small screen flashing.

Mena.

Lacey pressed the green button and lifted the phone to her ear.

"Holly, my god—"

"Mena, it's... it's Lacey."

Mena's sudden crying outburst drew forth tears of Lacey's own.

"Mitch... Mitch is... god, I can't even... they... they found him, Lacey."

Lacey tried to speak, but nothing came out. Mena growled, "Why isn't Holly *ever* here when I need her?" There was knocking over Mena's sobbing. "The police are here. I have to go."

The line went dead.

Lacey sat the device on the chair's plumply padded arm. The Qantas wallet had spilled onto the floor, and Lacey reached for it. She checked over her shoulder to the bathroom door, then opened the pouch. She unfolded the document stapled inside. The ticket was genuine enough, but Lacey was stunned by the date. Nestled in the folds of the expired itinerary, was a keycard from the Quest Shepparton hotel.

Holly came out of the bathroom, dressed professionally for her 'out-of-state' meeting. She took one look at Lacey, and her cheery façade vanished quicker than a raindrop on a thirsty desert plain.

Lacey croaked, "They found Mitch." Holly's mouth dropped open. Lacey added mutely, "He's dead, Holly."

"What? *No.* No, that... that can't be."

"It was just on the radio. Mena called."

Holly's eyes darted to her handbag, and then back to Lacey, who slipped from the Gucci knockoff the air ticket. She waved it and said, "You haven't been catching the redeye at all, have you? You've been carrying this old ticket around as nothing more than a prop. What's in Shepparton, Holly?"

"Lace." Holly came a step closer.

Lacey barked, "Don't."

Holly froze.

Lacey threw the ticket on the chair, then crossed her arms. "They say Mitch has only just died, not more than twenty-four hours. They suggest he was being held *captive.*"

"Lace, I know what you're thinking—"

"Tell me I'm wrong." Was it guilt that wet Holly's thick lashes? Was it grief? Or was it all *fake*? The crocodile tears of yet *another* master pretender. "I knew you were hiding something from me. But I ignored it because I..."

"Lace..."

"I don't know what this is – just what *exactly* it is you've been doing – but your brother-in-law is dead, and the police are all over it."

"Lace, I—"

"I can't be party to this. If I don't go to the police, they'll suspect I knew. I can hear them now, wondering how I could've been so... so *blind.* Twice!" Lacey's last word boomed.

"I..." Holly's voice broke. "I didn't want to lie to you, Lace. And I certainly didn't mean to hurt you." Again, she tried an approach.

Lacey howled, "Don't! Just... don't."

Holly's shoulders slumped. "There *is* an explanation."

Lacey looked down over her staunchly folded arms to her bare feet. "Explain to the police." She looked up again, because Holly deserved at least that, but her voice tremored, "They're on their way."

Holly wiped her streaked cheeks, an action made wholly redundant by a fresh onslaught of tears. Lacey couldn't breathe for her own misery.

Holly said softly, "I guess the light's not going to make its triumphant return after all."

Lacey looked away as Holly collected her things. She sensed Holly waiting for a reprieve, but Lacey couldn't give it. Instead, she closed her stinging, blurry, salt-sea eyes.

She didn't open them again until she heard the front door close.

Then she doubled over and wailed.

It was reported two hours later that Holly Dunham had surrendered to police.

* * *

22nd December, 1995

Lacey sat across the table from Holly, self-conscious, and guilty for the smile Holly gave her.

Lacey said, "Thank you for agreeing to see me."

"It's so wonderful you're here, Lace."

Lacey had prepared for the meeting by telling herself she would not get emotional, but Holly's easy forgiveness made her immediately misty-eyed. "I'm sorry it's taken me so long to get here."

"You've been overseas helping your grandmother. I understand. I'm so sorry about your pop."

"He's at peace."

Holly nodded. Then she smiled. "You look good."

Lacey replied, "So do you."

Holly laughed. It was an honest, uninhibited bellow, and it prompted Lacey's own genuine chuckle.

But then Holly's pleasure receded, replaced by a pain that Lacey felt deep down to her core.

Lacey said, "I'm so sorry, Holly."

"Don't be sorry. I wanted it to be over. The truth needed to come out."

"I... I should've let you explain."

With that, Holly did. "I'm sure you know about the affair." Lacey now knew about *all* of it. Mena had told her everything. Holly's cheeks turned pink. "It was brief, not more than a couple of weeks before I put a stop to it. Mitch was angry, but I thought he'd accepted it. Afterwards, things got strange. I felt like I was being watched. I'd wake up in the middle of the night to weird noises. I'd find things in the house out of place. I started receiving threatening letters, late night phone calls where the caller would just *breathe* at me. One morning I found the tyres on my car slashed. I should've gone to the police, but I knew it was him, and I didn't want Mena to find out about us.

It was a week after Mitch went missing that Mena told me their bank accounts had been drained. Mitch had taken everything and left her with a mountain of debt. A few weeks later, Mitch contacted me.

He demanded I see him; threatened that if I didn't do as he said, Mena would pay. So I did; at the shack outside of Shepparton. I thought I could appeal to his sense of... *decency*, but he was fuming. We struggled and I... I hit him in the head with a vodka bottle. There was a *lot* of blood. I couldn't just leave him like it, so I tied him up and treated him until he recovered. I didn't know what to do with him after that. Every time I went there to tend to his needs, he screamed at me that when he got loose, he would kill me; *and* Mena. I didn't see a way out. The last night you and I spent together, I'd decided to tell Mena and the police everything. Of course, *he* decided to have a heart attack.

It's a matter of public record now, but I wanted you to hear it from me."

"Holl, I am... I'm so sorry. About all of it."

"It's okay. Really. I'm okay. I'm ashamed more than anything."

Lacey shook her head. "Mena doesn't blame you, Holly. She told me you warned her from the beginning about him."

"She told you that?" Lacey nodded. Holly slumped in the chair. "He was always so *charming*. She was caught in his spell, but I knew there was something off about him. Then they got married and I had to make my peace with it. Everything was fine for a while. But then he... he turned his attention on me, and I knew... I knew saying no to him might be dangerous. I've made so many mistakes, Lace, but he proved me right about that." Lacey offered her hand.

Holly took it and said, "You know, when all this started, you were the only reporter who didn't present Mitch as some kind of saint."

"Maybe that's because in the beginning, you were the only one ballsy enough to be honest with me about him. I don't know if you're aware, but others are now coming forward with similar stories about Mitch Gordon. It seems he was quite the bully."

Holly nodded, then steered a gaze towards the barred windows, bright with midday light.

Lacey asked, "Do you know what today is?"

"Three sleeps till..." Holly's voice suddenly broke, and she started to weep. She brushed both her eyes and cursed, "God! I promised myself I wouldn't do this. I'm sorry."

"Hey." Lacey propped both hands on the table, face up. Holly at first hesitated. But then she drifted her own hands down, and their fingers locked. Lacey said softly, "It's the summer solstice. The time of year when the sun is highest, the day is longest, and the night... the night is *short*, Holly." Holly's face broke into a most precious smile. Lacey said, "I know I haven't been here for you, but I'm back now. I'll come visit you *every* week. The next twelve months will pass, and then you'll be free.

And there'll be someone waiting for you, under the mistletoe and with a boatload of presents. That is, if you'll have me."

Holly beamed. She kissed Lacey's fingers, and then she laughed through tears, and for Lacey (*'This is my fairy-tale, right here, Holly Dunham.'*), it was the most beautiful, most treasurable moment in the world.

11

Write a story about a first or last kiss.

THE WAR OUTSIDE

One

F ebruary 14
14:02

Yet another nearby explosion rocked the ward. Every person in the debris-strewn corridor ducked simultaneously, as if they were all members of the same badly dressed ballet. All except Jess, who was being shipped on the gurney with the squeaky castors, and who flinched so violently her cannula might've popped.

Tehani, the raven-haired, olive-skinned, thirty-year-old nurse, straightened and stroked Jess's cheek. "Are you okay?" Jess nodded. Tehani offered with trademark calm, "Okay, let's get you back to your room."

Once there and settled with her infernal tubes, Jess asked, "Do you think they'll hit the hospital?"

Tehani attached Jess to the monitor via the finger clip and replied, "Of course not. They wouldn't be so stupid. There are rules, even though I know right now it doesn't feel like it. Not to us plebs, anyway."

"What... what about the ambulance?"

"What ambulance?"

"I heard an ambulance was stopped on the way here. I... I heard the rebels..." *Shit.* Jess couldn't even say the words. The very idea was just too heinous.

Tehani's dark eyes fired. "Who told you about that?"

"I overheard people talking in the corridor."

BOOM!

Tehani lurched over Jess like a protective hen.

The windows rattled like old bones.

Dust coughed from the ceiling like death ashes.

The rumble faded, and Jess let go her breath.

Tehani warily rose.

Jess whispered, "Are we okay?"

Tehani flicked the debris off her shoulders. "We're okay, Fielding."

Jess scanned the room. The floor had become a resting place for bloodied clothes, a lonely shoe, discarded surgical gloves, a toppled chair, and a well-spread splatter that had aged to a ghoulish mahogany. The pattern of that stain – the violence with which the fluid had so obviously been thrust – prompted a sense of doom that up until that moment, Jess had been able to gag.

Tehani flitted to the window and looked down through the buckled blinds.

Jess asked, "What do you see down there?"

"I... nothing." The blind flicked closed with the removal of Tehani's tapered fingers, shutting out an eerie orange glow. She turned with a complexion more peaked than Jess had ever seen it, prompting Jess to a quiet cuss. "Shit."

"Hey, Fielding. We're fine here. We'll be okay."

Jess wanted to believe her, and although she didn't doubt Tehani's desperate need for the appearance of sincerity, there was a fracture in her voice that made Jess shudder.

A feeling of impending disaster prompted a poorly timed question that Jess had no business asking. "Why didn't you marry Tane?"

Tehani darted a side-glance to the window. "You know there's a war going on outside, right?" Jess should've apologised for asking. But she wanted an answer. She'd wanted an answer for a good six months.

Tehani slipped a stray lock of hair behind her ear. Then she drifted to Jess's side. "I... the truth is, I was thinking about someone else. I was ashamed, but I... I couldn't stop it. It wasn't right, or fair, so I called it off."

"Someone else?" Tehani nodded. Jess asked, "Did you ever have a discussion with this *someone else*?"

Tehani's plump lips thinned, and she scratched her elbow. "No."

"Why not?"

"I don't think this is the—"

"Why not, Tee?"

Tehani expunged a quiet sigh and looked up at the cracked ceiling. "Okay. I never approached them because I thought they were interested in someone else."

"You *thought*?"

"It's what I was told, anyway."

"It's what you were... you didn't go to them?"

"The last thing I wanted was to come between this guy and the... the amazing woman he found."

This guy.

Jess didn't want to feel gut-punched by that, and under the circumstances, maybe it was wrong of her. But it was the circumstance that was driving an overwhelming sense of panic that this might be the last time she ever got to be completely honest.

Jess asked, "Is this amazing woman draping herself over patients in a hospital ward in the middle of a war zone?"

"If you're talking about what I did just now, I had a stomach cramp."

"Ohhh. Stomach cramp."

"You don't think I was protecting you, surely."

"Pfft. No."

"Because I find you, for the most part, extremely annoying."

"You're in good company."

"Like your mother's?"

"Anything she says about me that is south of glowing praise is a flat-out lie."

Tehani gave a smiling side-eye. "She says she'd hand you to the rebels herself if she didn't think they'd palm you straight back."

Jess cackled. "Well, that much is probably true." Tehani grinned a perfect set of teeth. It was a relief to see; a gifted radiance in a pit of darkness.

Tehani straightened the blanket over Jess's legs, tucked her in and then fluffed her pillow. While she was tending, she said, "We're going to get through this, Jess Fielding. You're going to get well, and then I'm going to take you clothes shopping."

Clothes shopping. How far would they have to travel for that, now that much of their city had been razed?

Despite the bleak thought, Jess asked, "What's wrong with my wardrobe?"

Tehani cocked an eyebrow. "You have tops in there older than Jesus. I'm betting knickers too."

"Hey, *I* dress for comfort."

"Yeah, well, you can join the rest of us and suffer in tight jeans and five-inch heels."

"No corsets?"

Tehani chuckled. As she smoothed a hand over Jess's hair, a young doctor appeared out the corner of Jess's eye. He rushed past, then backed up and stood at the door in his dirty white coat and blue jeans and mussed black curls.

"Nurse Imar," he said. "Can I talk to you out here for a moment?"

"Of course, Doctor." Tehani clutched Jess's hand. "I'll be right back."

Jess nodded, and watched with trepidation as Tehani disappeared from the room.

* * *

Tehani returned moments later and swiftly erected one rail of the gurney.

Jess asked, "What's going on?"

Tehani replied without looking at her, "You're being evacuated."

"What?"

Tehani circled hastily to the other side of the cot and lifted the second rail. "Everyone who can be transported is being relocated."

"To where?"

"I'm not sure. Hopefully another hospital."

"Wh... why?"

Tehani removed the clip from Jess's finger and finally made eye contact. "Now is not the time for questions, Fielding."

"What about you? Are you coming?"

"There are patients here who can't be moved. I need to stay."

"Well, then, I'm staying too."

"No, you're not."

Two men rushed into the room and hijacked both ends of the gurney. Jess hollered, "No!"

Tehani laid a palm on Jess's shoulder. "Jess, honey, Rem and Teek will take care of you. You'll be safe with them."

Jess roared, "I'm not leaving!"

The men unlocked the castors with their scuffed sandshoes.

Jess wrenched at the cannula.

Tehani wrestled her hands. "What are you doing, Jess? Stop this!"

"I'm not leaving!"

The older of the two men warned, "There's not a lot of time."

Tehani cupped Jess's jaw with both hands. "Listen to me. As soon as I can, I'll come and find you."

Jess cried, "Please, Tee. Don't let them take me."

Tehani quivered, "I'll come and find you. And then we'll have that discussion. Okay?"

The gurney squeaked, and Tehani's reassuring touch fell away.

Tehani's inference only intensified Jess's fright at being separated from her. She begged, "Tee, please. Please, don't send me away."

Tehani's hands flew to her mouth, and tears rushed her cheeks.

It was the last Jess saw of her before she was hurried on squealing wheels from the room.

* * *

Despite the clattering windows and falling plaster, the gurney didn't stop, except for the scuffling wounded who were heading in the same direction.

Through a blur, Jess made out a splash of colour bumping against the ceiling. She wiped away tears, and into sharp focus came a vision of two heart-shaped balloons. It only occurred to her then, the date, and the hospital's gift shop coming up on the left.

Jess muttered, "Stop."

The young man, Rem, retorted, "We can't stop, Miss. The transport can't wait."

Jess implored, "Please, I don't want to go. I'm not—"

BOOM!

The deafening blast opened a hell portal, with a hurricane at its centre and a rage of shrapnel at its extremity. Amid a calamitous shaking and a fierce wind, Jess's face and arms were torn like wet paper. A ferocious energy toppled the gurney and crashed it to the floor, and Jess spewed out of it onto a bed of glass and rubble. Choking on a cloud of dust and with her ears ringing, she lifted her head. Rem was sprawled flat, looking at her but not *seeing* her. A chunk of his skull was missing.

Sobbing and bleeding, Jess pulled herself across the floor. Through the gift shop's open door, a jumble of stock had been shaken off the shelves, and the white tile was littered with teddy bears, stick-balloons, and brightly-hued petals severed from their stems. A card-stand had been tossed, and a bunch of pens strewn. Jess slithered forward, oblivious of the sticky red streak marking her trail.

Two

Tehani wiped her face. She could hear Jess crying in the corridor, and couldn't bring herself to leaving the room until the sound of the woman's trauma faded out of earshot.

Sending Jess away was hard, but there was no other choice. The hospital – to Tehani's disillusionment – was no longer a haven. Instead, both healthcare worker and patient had become pawns in a soulless, political tug-of-war. She had not thought she would ever see this day. But it was here. It was real. All the rules she had until then prayed would not fail, had been abandoned.

All of these innocent people.

What would happen to them now?

And Jess.

Her darling Jess.

Tehani was no happier for letting her go than Jess was for leaving.

Being parted from her.

Not just parted. Allowing Jess to be forcibly taken.

Having no idea where she was going.

Having no clue whether or not her medical needs would elsewhere be met.

Never having told Jess how she felt.

Afraid for reasons that before seemed important, but now...

BOOM!

Tehani was knocked off her feet. Whole chunks of ceiling thumped against the littered floor. The lights flickered. Screams echoed. Tehani launched off her belly and darted into the corridor, into a stampede of terrified civilians. Tehani knew for sure then that the hospital had been hit. As if that realisation weren't frightening enough, Tehani remembered what she'd seen out the window.

She whispered, "Jess."

Then she ran.

* * *

Tehani came upon an alarming scene. A hole had been punched into the side of the building, and she could see past cables and beams and insulate to the neighbouring war-torn structure. In the hallway before her, among the rubble, was the toppled gurney. Teek was on the floor, propped on an elbow and rubbing his crown.

Tehani dropped on a knee by his side. "Teek, are you alright?"

He looked up at her with red-eyed confusion. "I... I'm not sure. What happened?"

"We were hit. Teek, where is Jess?"

"I... I don't know. What about Rem?"

Tehani leaned to her left and looked past the wheels of the gurney to a grim sight. Between she and Rem on the floor, there was blood that couldn't have been his.

Tehani asked, "Can you stand?"

"I..."

Tehani rose and gripped his arm. "Teek, come on. You need to get up." With her help, Teek got to his feet. She held his shoulders and directed, "You need to find some place to hide."

"*Hide?*"

The sound of automatic gunfire startled them both.

Teek muttered, "Oh shit."

Tehani shook him and said, "Go. Hide."

"Why are they doing this?"

But the why didn't matter; not to Rem, nor to the thousands of others who had already perished; and in the face of Tehani's own mortality, it didn't matter to her either. "Teek, go."

"What are you gonna do?"

"I have to find Jess."

"I'll help you."

"Go, Teek! Find somewhere to hole up and don't come out." With a grey expression, Teek backed away. Then he spun and bolted.

Tehani turned her attention to the blood that tracked across the gift shop's threshold. She rushed in to find among a clutter of giftware and broken flowers, Jess on her belly on the floor. Tehani dropped to her knees and draped a hand on Jess's shoulder. Jess's face was turned to her, but her eyes were closed.

"Jess." The woman's pale skin was dotted with cuts and abrasions. Tehani pressed two fingers to Jess's carotid. "Jess, can you hear me?" A pair of eyes opened, prompting Tehani's emphatic sigh of relief.

Jess mumbled, "Tee."

"I'm here."

Ratatatatat!

Tehani muttered, "They're coming."

"Was… was that…?"

"Can you move?"

Jess brought her hands level with her shoulders. She pressed up only a fraction, and cried out in pain.

Tehani said, "Okay. It's okay. Listen, I'm going to step out for just a second. I'll be right back. I'm not leaving you, you got it?" Jess nodded. Tehani bolted from the shop, leaned over Rem's body and dragged him from his own bloody pool to the threshold. She left him there, stepped back into the shop and closed the door. She couldn't do better without the key.

Jess had rolled over, revealing among other wounds, a blood-soaked abdomen. She was clutching a pink envelope to her chest. Tehani kneeled and pressed a palm to a clammy forehead.

Ratatatatat!

Jess gasped.

Tehani brushed her cheek. "We'll get through this. Now listen up. I'm going to drag you behind the counter and we're going to be very quiet there. Okay?" Jess clutched the envelope tighter. Tehani assured, "I don't want to take that from you, Fielding. But I do need you to give me your hands." Jess nodded and relinquished the treasure, and Tehani stuffed it in the back of her pants. Then she gripped Jess's offered paws and dragged her through the debris to the other side of the counter. Satisfied they were out of sight, she stroked Jess's brow. "Don't go anywhere." Jess managed a strained smile. Tehani scavenged from the scattered inventory a cluster of soft toys, then swept cards and debris over the bloody trail Jess had oozed. Then she returned to Jess's side.

Jess murmured, "Teddies? That's really sweet."

"You think so?" Tehani lifted Jess's shoulders and placed a pink zebra behind her head, then tore into the seam of a defenceless blue dog and pulled the stuffing from it. She raised Jess's shirt and pressed the canine's innards to a weeping puncture wound. Jess winced. Tehani winked. "Sweet. That's me."

"Just so you know, I'll be filing a complaint about you. Nurse Imar, the sadist."

"Honestly, I think it's a prerequisite Have you met Nurse Watson?"

Jess's chuckle became a grimace, became a sudden, quiet desperation. "Tee, there's something... there's something I need to –"

Ratatatatatatat!

The sound was close.

They were on the ward.

They were coming.

Tehani lifted her eyes over the counter, and looked through the shattered windows into the corridor.

Two men in black garb appeared, with rifles at their hips.

Three

Tehani ducked and planted a finger-V over Jess's mouth.

Jess smoothed her blood-crusted digits over Tehani's hand.

Click.

The typically benign sound of a door latch raised the hairs on the back of Tehani's neck.

The red whites of Jess's eyes swelled. Four hands laced tightly together.

Trooper One muttered, "See somethin'?"

No reply.

"Hey, jackass. What are you lookin' at?"

"Tehani Imar."

"What's a Tehani Imar?"

The sound of paper flicking.

Trooper One huffed, "Did you find something or not?"

Trooper Two chortled. "Listen to this.
I understand why you sent me away.
You want me to be safe.
It's my fault you don't know:
My safe place is with you.
It's my mistake you don't see:
I'd rather stare down the Devil himself by your side,
than be sheltered from hell away from you.
I'm so sorry I haven't told you.
Please, God, don't let it be too late."

Jess's perspiring brow knotted. Her jaw clenched. Her alert jasper eyes were begging. Tehani patted the small of her back to confirm the envelope was gone.

Trooper One scoffed, "Alright, jackass. You give it a tug while *I* do the sweep. Happy Valentine's Day."

This was it. This might've been all the time Tehani had left, and if it were so, then she had been gifted an opportunity to make at least one thing right; to do the one thing she wished she'd done so much sooner.

Tehani leaned over Jess and tenderly smoothed the woman's cheek. Jess caressed Tehani's jaw with unsteady fingers, and the smile Tehani received then – no matter the sorrow behind it – filled Tehani with an overwhelming sense of gratitude. Tehani swallowed a sob, and placed a delicate kiss on Jess's soft lips.

The two were joined that way when the clomp of heavy boots came lazily towards them.

12

Set your entire story in a car.

RUNAWAY AND SKYE

(The Dimming of the Light, Pt 2)

Sunday, 10 July, 2033
16:59

When Skye Simmons pulled her Tesla into Springvale's Botanical Cemetery, she expected she'd have to make a trek on foot through the gardens to Tyler Devereaux's gravesite. But as she drew nearer to Tyler's final resting place, she spotted Millie's chestnut pigtails waiting for her on the curb of the narrow road. She pulled over, leaned across and flung the passenger door open. Millie dropped her pink backpack into the footwell and climbed in. Then she fidgeted in her lap.

"Millie, honey, what are you doing out here alone in the freezing cold?"

"I wanted to talk to Mama Tyler about something."

"Oh, honey, you're ten years old. I'm sure your mum would've brought you here if you'd asked."

"But I didn't want her to hear."

"Then you call *me*, kiddo. You don't go venturing out on your own."

Millie looked at her with her big blue eyes. "You didn't tell her I called you, did you?"

Without giving a yay or a nay, Skye asked, "Whose phone did you use?"

"Macy's."

"Who is Macy?"

"She's visiting her friend, Brenda. Brenda saved her life."

"How did Brenda do that, honey?"

"Macy was very sick. Brenda gave her a kidney."

"Oh, wow. That's a beautiful gift."

Millie looked out the window, then waved enthusiastically at a woman sitting under a tree. The woman smiled and waved back. Skye gestured her own *thank you*, then reached into the back seat and retrieved a blanket so that she might spread it over Millie's lap.

"Okay, let's get you home and warm, devil-child."

As Skye pulled the car out of the cemetery onto the main road, Millie asked, "Skye, can you miss someone you never met?"

"Do you miss your mama?" Skye stole a look at the glum young lady and caught sight of a nod. "Well then, there's your answer."

"But how? My friend, Candace, says I can't. I never knew her, so I can't miss her."

Skye slowed down with the traffic, then stopped at a set of red lights. "What are some things your Mama Tyler liked to do?"

Millie twisted the cord of her jacket. Then she looked up and said, "I know she liked to paint. And she was a really good drawer."

"What else?"

"Um… I know she was smart. She was an architect."

"I think she was probably *very* smart, just like her baby girl." Millie grinned. Skye asked, "What else?"

"I think she was kind. Mummy only likes kind people."

"That's some spot-on reasoning, kiddo."

"She liked ice-cream. And chocolate. And funny movies. Oh, and books."

"What was her favourite ice-cream?"

Millie chuckled. "Mum says she liked rainbow Paddlepops."

Skye laughed. "I like banana."

"And her favourite movie was Steel Magnolias."

"Oh, I love that movie!"

"Me too! Maybe you and me and mum can watch it together. Tonight!"

"We'll see." Skye gave the young girl's knee a pat. "See? You *do* know your mama. Don't let anyone ever tell you you can't miss her, Millie. Your feelings are your own. If you miss your mama, then you miss her, plain and simple."

Millie turned her face away and murmured, "My mum misses her."

Skye said softly, "I know, honey. They loved each other very much."

"That's why I wanted to talk to Mama today."

"Is it okay if I ask what you talked with her about?"

Millie nodded. "I know she was smart, so I knew she would get it. And I know she was kind, so I knew she wouldn't be mad."

"Mad about what, angel?"

"About letting Mum love someone else."

Millie fell silent then, and stared out the passenger window at the tree-lined street whizzing by, with the lights of buildings growing bolder as the sun dipped below the skyline.

Skye thought back to the day she and Lexi had met. Before that, they had communicated via video phone. Skye was a police officer stationed in Sydney, and involved in the investigation of the car crash that had so tragically taken Tyler's life. That was July 2023, almost ten years ago to the day. Lexi and Skye had soon after met during one of Skye's visits to Melbourne, and she remembered all too well how broken Lexi had still been over her partner's death. Skye doubted she would ever feel as strongly for anyone, as Lexi obviously had for Tyler. As a result, Skye stopped falling into women's beds, and focused solely on her career.

As time went on the two women lost touch, but Skye had never forgotten about Lexi. In '28, Skye successfully applied for the Victoria Police Critical Incident Response Team. She bought a house on a lake, and once settled into her new surrounds, reached out. Lexi had seemed genuinely pleased to hear from her, and a friendship had blossomed that for Skye would become something more. She had tried to ignore them, but her feelings grew. They were feelings she didn't know were mutual, and she didn't want to rob Lexi of anything else when the woman had already lost so much.

Skye handed Millie the phone from the console and said, "Why don't you call your mum? I'm sure she's worried sick about you."

Millie turned the device in her small hands. "I think mum's looking for another place for us to live." The dear child dropped her chin to her chest.

Skye said, "Are you sure, honey? She hasn't mentioned anything to me."

Millie shrugged. "I don't want to go. If we move, I can't take my unicorns. Mama Tyler designed them for me."

Unnerved herself by the possibility, Skye downplayed her alarm. "I'm sure if Mum is thinking about moving, she has a very good reason."

"What if we move so far away that you can't visit?"

"Well, honey, you'd have to move a long, long way away for me to not come visit."

"Can I tell you something?"

"Anything, kiddo."

"You have to promise not to tell her."

"Well now, that depends."

"Please, Skye."

Skye merged into a right-turning lane, and stopped on the demand of the red arrow. "Okay, I promise. What is it?"

"When you visit us, Mum smiles and laughs more than she ever does with anyone else. But when you leave, she goes quiet. And then I think she gets sad."

Skye swallowed a lump. "Millie, honey—"

"I think she wants to be happy, but I think she's scared it will make Mama Tyler *un*happy. So I wanted to ask Mama Tyler if that was true: if my mum being happy would make her sad."

"What do you think her answer was?"

"I think Mama Tyler loved my mum so much, that she would never, ever want to see her be sad."

Millie's concern had played on Skye's own mind, if not in quite the same terms.

Skye said, "Do you remember the first summer your mum brought you to my house on the lake?" Millie nodded. "Do you remember the paddle boats?"

Millie's mouth opened wide. "Yes!" She added matter-of-factly, "I had very much fun."

"Do you remember how we took you to those boats every day?"

"I was scared at first."

"You *were* scared. But every day we walked you down to the water and asked if you wanted to give it a try. You saw the fun the other kids were having, and you knew we were going to be right there with you. And so, on the fifth day, you finally said yes."

"I sat between you and Mum."

"And you splashed us every chance you got."

Millie giggled. "I wasn't scared anymore."

"No, you weren't scared anymore. You were very brave. Your mum didn't take you out on that boat until you decided you were ready. She knew that eventually you *would* be, in your own time." Skye didn't know if Millie would understand, but she could see the cogs turning behind those intelligent eyes.

Millie surprised her then. "But I wouldn't ever have done it if I didn't know I was allowed. Mum had to tell me it was okay first."

Skye thought on it, and was dumbstruck. She couldn't know if Millie had realised what she'd said, but out of the mouth of babes had come a simple truth that had somehow wiggled out of Skye's line-of-sight. "You know what, kiddo? Your mama Tyler would be very impressed with your brain. But there is something you need to remember. Whatever your mum decides, it isn't just for her. It's for both of you. She has to do what she thinks is best for *you*, Millie. You're her number one priority. You know what that means, right?"

"She's my number one pri-om... pri-lom... pri-bobbity, as well."

Skye curbed a chuckle. "Oh, honey, I can see that. Perhaps you should tell her when I get you home. In the meantime," Skye reached across and gave Millie's hand a squeeze. Then she said, "Jukebox, please play The Unicorn Song by The Irish Rovers."

The delightful tune played, Skye tweaked the volume, and Millie squealed with glee.

* * *

It was after six and dark when Skye pulled the car up at the house. The front door burst open, and Lexi came rushing down the footpath with a puffer jacket in hand. Her long dark hair was tied back, but her dishevelled fringe hinted at a ruffled psyche. Millie climbed out, and Lexi threw the garment over the little runaway's shoulders. Then she bobbed and took Millie in her arms.

"Millie Banks-Devereaux, don't you ever, *ever* disappear like that again."

"I'm sorry, Mummy."

Skye retrieved the backpack from the footwell, then climbed out of the car and circled to the two ladies.

Lexi glanced up at her while she cupped Millie's puffy cheeks. "Where have you been, young lady?"

"With Mama."

"And how did you get to Mama?"

"I... I stole the card from your purse. I caught the bus."

"Oh my g... *why*? Why would you do that? You know if you want to go visit your mama, I will take you *any* time. I'll always take you."

"I know, Mummy. I'm sorry."

Lexi's head lolled, losing Skye the sight of a profuse worry. After a few moments she raised it again, and revealed a restraint that probably, at least, convinced Millie. "How much was the bus fare?"

Millie fished in her pocket and handed Lexi the card. "Fifty-two dollars."

Lexi took it and said, "You're going to have to work it off with chores, you know that."

"Yes, Mummy."

Lexi wiped her own pale cheek. "Go on, inside with you, scallywag. And wash your hands, okay? I'm about to serve dinner."

"Mummy?"

"Yes, Millie."

"You're my *priority*." Millie threw her arms around Lexi's neck. "I love you, Mummy."

Lexi hugged her tight and sobbed, "I love you too, baby."

Then Millie turned and hugged Skye's midriff. She muffled into Skye's belly, "I love you, Skye."

Skye leaned over and kissed the young lady's crown. "I love you too, kiddo. Now go on, do as your mother says. I'll stop by someday soon for that movie you promised me."

Millie smiled, relieved Skye of the backpack and ran inside.

With her arms across her chest, Lexi stepped close. "Thank you so much for picking her up. *And* for calling me. I was so worried."

"I cancelled the police report."

"Thank you. I just... I don't understand. She's never done anything like this before."

Skye touched Lexi's elbow. "Hey. She's okay, I promise you."

"Did she tell you what was so urgent that she couldn't wait for me to run her out there?"

"I think... I think ultimately it comes down to a little girl wanting both her mums to be happy."

"I don't... I'm not sure I understand."

Skye looked over Lexi's shoulder to the modest three-bed red-brick, a house that had felt more like a home to her than her own sprawling lakeside manor. "Is it true you're thinking about moving?"

"Well, the idea is only new. I... I hadn't thought about it seriously. And it's not that I particularly want to. Did she talk about that?"

"She's worried she can't take her unicorns. But I think it's more than that. I think... I think she thinks you're running away."

"*Running away*? From what, exactly?"

"I think... I think she thinks you're running away from *me*."

Lexi's jaw stiffened. Then her eyes fell. She unfolded her arms and shoved her hands in the back of her jeans. "Why on earth would she think that?"

Skye whispered, "Do you want me to answer honestly?"

Lexi again crossed her arms in front, looking more nervous than Skye had ever seen her. "I wish you would."

Skye's own anxiety was particularly robust when she replied, "I think Millie knows I love you." Lexi's expression didn't change. But there was more emotion in those eyes than could be contained. Skye said, "I'm not telling you because I expect anything from you. It's just... it's the simple truth. And I really didn't want to walk away from you one more day, without telling it. When I'm with you, everything feels right. And when I'm not, it just... it just *doesn't*. I love you, Lexi, and I love your daughter, and if you don't feel the same way about me, I still want us to be friends. I don't want to take *anything* away from you. Ever."

Lexi said nothing. She just stared with those unblinking eyes.

Skye steeled her bottom lip. "I should... I should go. I'm sorry, Lexi." Skye turned with every intention of rushing to her car and not looking back.

A little voice cried, "Skye! Skye, wait!" Skye slowly faced them.

Lexi quickly wiped her cheeks, then lifted Millie into her arms. "What is it, noisy girl?"

"I found Steel Magnolias. Can Skye stay and watch it with us?"

Skye said, "Another time, kiddo. I... I have some work waiting for me."

Lexi lowered Millie to the ground and said, "Stay. I haven't had a good dose of *Ouiser* sarcasm for as long as I can remember."

"Oh, no. I couldn't. You guys are about to have dinner, and I really—"

Millie interrupted. "Mummy, are we really moving?"

Lexi smoothed her daughter's hair. "I think we should stay, don't you?"

Millie hissed, "Yes."

Lexi looked to Skye and said, "Stay. I made lasagne. From scratch."

Millie squealed, "Yes!"

Lexi offered timidly, "There's plenty to go around. There's even enough for seconds if you're hungry. And I think... I think there might be some wine in the cupboard." Skye was as bereft of word as Lexi had seemed only moments before. Lexi came close and reached low for Skye's hand. She whispered, "Stay. Please. Maybe later I'll get around to showing you how *I* feel."

Skye had no intention of further denying the request. Millie took Skye's free hand, and together the three of them left the cold of the night, for the warmth of a home.

13

This next story is not based on a prompt.
It is rather the beginning of the everlasting friendship that formed the
heart and soul of my debut novel, Cicatrice: New Eyes and Brave.
How Mel and Jamie first met is briefly touched upon in the novel, but I
publish the full retelling here, for new readers as well as 'old reliables'.
To the collective, I offer my sincerest gratitude.
Your support is priceless.

INDIGO AND
THE BULLY

Melbourne, Australia

January 29th 2005
6:08pm

Bec looked stunning as usual. With her long auburn hair styled to perfection and her black dress hugging her athletic curves, it was no surprise young men were constantly tripping over their tongues in her presence. Jamie of the blonde tresses was gowned in white, and the two stood together in the ballroom like opposing chess pieces: bickering.

"Oh, look!" Bec gestured with a nod to Richard Barkley. "He's had a crush on you since seventh grade. Are you telling me he's never once asked you out?"

"Richard and I are *friends*. Dating him would be like... Frodo dating Samwise."

Bec snorted. "Those two halflings have more chemistry than Michael Dee and Cathy Zee."

"Huh. Why are you so interested in my love life, anyway?"

"*Interest* is a misnomer. How can I be interested in a thing that doesn't exist?"

"Good point. Shouldn't you be concentrating on your own dalliances?"

Bec's sigh was almost a groan. "I'm waiting on Archer to tire of Phoebe. Four months and he's still drooling. I'll triumph in the end though. She'll age badly. Then I'll make my move."

"Patience is a bitter plant, but it has a sweet fruit."

Bec chuckled. "Alright, Confucius. If not Dick, then who? Point someone out to me. There are a lot of handsome guys here this evening."

"I'm not here looking for my soul mate, Bec Bradbury. I'm only here because you dragged me out of my nice comfy chair."

"Oh, come on. Mum and dad would've been pissed at me if I'd left you at the flat."

"There are a thousand guests here. They wouldn't have noticed if I'd spent the night in with a good book and a tub of Haagen-Dazs."

"Just humour me and pick someone already."

Jamie clicked her tongue. Then she scanned the plethora of suits and tuxedos that had sorted themselves into cliques, like penguins chattering amongst their respective waddles. Through a gap she spied a new face, not in a suit but in a simply elegant indigo gown. Her jet black hair fell over her bare light-brown shoulders, and silver hoop earrings dangled from hidden ears. She was holding a clutch in both hands and looking somewhat awkward. The woman conducted her own scan and caught Jamie in a stare.

Propriety should've seen Jamie to looking away. Instead, their eyes locked, and the woman's fine features turned from mild discomfort to subtle curiosity. Jamie smiled at her. But it wasn't just a smile of politeness. Something about the vision genuinely pleased her. The woman smiled back, and in that moment, Jamie knew they had to meet.

Jamie turned to Bec. "Hey, are you okay on your own for a few minutes?"

"No!" Bec latched onto her arm. "I need you here when—"

Conspicuously, the heads of a number of guests turned towards the bay windows that looked out over the well-manicured front garden, and some of the gathering moved in that direction.

Bec muttered, "What are they all on about?"

A holler came from outside. "Jamie!"

In the ensuing hush, several pairs of bewildered eyes found her. Jamie looked to her best friend, who returned a sympathetic gaze.

"Jamie!" Jamie jumped. Then she pushed through the gathering to the glass doors and stepped out onto the decking. The rich colours of seasonal blooms painted an otherwise pleasant picture, sullied by Alex tripping into a bed of beauteous begonias.

Jamie looked over her shoulder, humiliated that everyone was gawking at her drunk father. Bec was amongst them, and after glimpsing Jamie with wide eyes, turned and disappeared into the pack.

Then Jamie saw her. That new face, standing right where Bec had just been. But she wasn't looking at Alex like the others. She was looking at Jamie.

Alex regained her attention with a grumble. "Dammit, Jamie. Do you even know what day it is?" He'd lifted himself out of the flowerbed, and was smoothing his dishevelled hair. He plucked a yellow petal from it and *threw down* like a petulant child.

"Yes, Alex. I know what day it is."

"Do you think your mother would want you here with these cocky-rich bastards, instead of your father?"

I think she'd want me anywhere you weren't. Jamie held her tongue. He came towards her, and although they were separated by several metres of lawn and a flight of stairs, Jamie stepped back.

Alex stumbled over the garden edging. "Fuck! Fuckin'... *shit!* Let's go, Jamie."

Jamie stammered, "I don't... I'm not..."

"Not what? Not sayin' *no* to me, is what."

Two men stormed out from behind her, and Jamie was relieved when she recognised the tuxedo, greying hairs and gold-rimmed specs of Mr Bradbury. His brother, Shane, was right behind him.

Mr Bradbury – Peter – pointed to the gate. "I've called the police. If you don't remove yourself from my property, Mr Stevens, they *will*."

"I'm not leavin' without Jamie."

"I'm afraid you are. Jamie is fine where she is."

Alex mumbled, "Prissy motherfucker." Then he hollered, "I mean it, Jamie!"

Jamie heard police sirens in the distance.

Peter ordered, "Leave. Now."

Alex puffed his chest like a blue-footed booby. He brushed his jumper with both hands, then grunted and turned away.

Peter pivoted to his inquisitive guests. "Nothing to see here, folks. Just a soul lost his way." Then he looked down at Jamie and placed a gentle hand on her arm. "Are you alright, Jamie darling?" Jamie nodded, and they both watched as Alex teetered through the open gates. Peter said to Shane, "Can you go make sure he's not driving?" Shane nodded and quietly followed Alex out.

Peter kissed Jamie's forehead. "I don't want this to spoil your evening. As far as I'm concerned, it's already forgotten."

Then Bec was by her side and wrapped her muscled swimmer's arm around Jamie's shoulder. Jamie peered through the window. Guests were losing interest and drifting away. But the new face – the one Jamie was looking for – had already disappeared.

* * *

Not twenty minutes later, Jamie was part of a circle of students with whom she'd already become acquainted. Most had the decency not to mention Jamie's shame. The same circumspection didn't apply to Tannen Granger, who seemed determined to wring every last bit of humiliation out of the ordeal.

"Shit, Jamie, *that's* your father? Christ, what a dick. I half expected he'd whip out his cock and start pissing on his own shoe."

Bec snapped, "Shut it, Tannen, for goodness' sake."

"I'm guessing that means you got your smarts from your mother. Although, fucking Christ, how smart could *she* have been?"

Bec scolded, "What the hell is wrong with you? If anyone here is being a dick, it's you."

He swatted the air. "Whatever, Bradbury." Courtney caught his eye, and his apparent interest in her was enough that he thankfully went in pursuit.

But it didn't end there. He had the good sense to wait until Bec was out of earshot, but every time Jamie found herself in his proximity, Tannen would make some backhand remark, some offensive jibe. Jamie had about had enough and was on the verge of leaving, when *Indigo* reappeared. She wafted gracefully to the drinks table, specifically to the punch bowl. Jamie watched as the young woman picked up a tumbler, took the ladle in hand and topped the glass with the blood-orange fizz. She met Jamie's gaze, then benched the full glass and started filling a second. She took both tumblers in hand, then summoned Jamie with no more than a brow lift. Jamie stifled a grin and went to her.

The woman greeted her with quiet charm. "I'm Vika."

"Vika."

"Well, *Mala*vika, actually. But that's a bit of a mouthful."

"I'm Jamie. It's nice to meet you, Vika."

"Jamie. I like that. Listen, Jamie, do you think you could hold onto these for a minute?" Vika offered the tumblers.

"Oh. Okay, sure." Jamie took them, then watched curiously as Vika placed her hands on the sides of the punch bowl. It wasn't overly large, but it was almost full when Vika lifted it carefully from the table. Jamie said, "What are you..."

Vika faced the crowd with it, then leaned close and muttered, "I'll be right back."

Jamie was enthralled by the majestic creature who strode surefootedly towards a particular group, of which Tannen was the loudest component. He was too busy guffawing to realise Vika was at his back, and one of his party obliged by pointing over his shoulder. When Tannen turned, he turned into a gushing waterfall of the Bradbury's own recipe *Hamilton Island* punch.

The stunned look on his soggy face – garnished with a slice of Tahitian lime – was so priceless that Jamie didn't know whether to clap or commiserate. His mates weren't so undecided, and exploded with laughter.

Vika said, "That's for taking the last pig-in-a-blanket. No gentleman worthy of that fine suit claims the last hors d'oeuvre." Jamie was muzzling her wide open mouth when Vika turned and gave her a wink. Jamie had no control then, over the grin that stretched from ear to ear, nor the laughter that immediately followed it.

* * *

Jamie and Vika found a quiet corner on the deck, and sat at a setting for two. Night had fallen, and the front garden was lit up with all the festivity of a mistimed Christmas.

Vika lifted the tumbler to her mischievously grinning lips. Jamie chuckled, and took a mouthful of the fruity beverage. Vika peered out over the gardens, and her look sobered under the spilling light. "So, ah... do you mind if I ask what the significance of today is?"

Jamie's smile dimmed. Not because she was opposed to the question. In fact, she was glad to talk about it. "It's my mother's birthday. She died when I was eight. Alex – my father – was driving the car. I..." Jamie stroked the base of her thumb with a finger. "I remember more of the accident than I'd like."

Vika asked softly, "Was he drunk then too?" They exchanged a sombre stare, and then Jamie let her eyes fall. She lifted them again to an intense study, and realised the woman she was so curious about had already glimpsed Jamie's deepest hurt.

Jamie said, "Tell me about you. How do you know the Bradbury's?"

"Well, actually, I..."

Determined heels thumped against the deck, and both women looked to a looming Peter Bradbury. He came towards them, and Vika stood.

Jamie launched out of the chair. "It's my fault, Mr Bradbury. Tannen was making some uncharitable remarks. I... Vika was just—"

Peter ignored her and demanded, "Who *are* you, young lady?"

Vika replied, "I'm... well, I just recently met your daughter on campus. I don't know anyone at the university, so she kindly invited me along."

"And as a thank you, you cause a ruckus by tipping a bowl of punch over the head of one of my guests?"

Jamie said, "Tannen was teasing; about Alex. He was being quite rude, honestly. Bec will tell you."

"Yes, she has been quite vocal about that. What the two of you – the *three* of you – fail to take into account, is that Tannen's own father is at present very ill. Tannen is quite upset, Miss Vika. What do you suppose I should do?"

Vika sighed. "You don't need to do anything, Mr Bradbury. I'll leave."

Jamie blurted, "No! That's not... that's not fair."

Peter raised a brow. "I'm surprised at you, Jamie. I don't tolerate frat-like stunts in my home."

Vika said, "It's okay, Jamie. I should go. Given the chance, I'd most certainly do it again." She smiled for Jamie, and sobered for Peter. "I'm sorry for Tannen's father. That doesn't mean he gets to shit all over the memory of Jamie's mother." Peter glanced at Jamie, then dropped his eye. Still, he didn't stop Vika from moving towards the deck stairs, or descending to the lush green lawn.

Peter said, "I'm sorry for Tannen's behaviour, Jamie. I'll speak to him."

Frustrated, Jamie left him and followed Vika into the brilliantly lit garden. Jamie called out as Vika made the gate, and Vika turned there. She held a subtle smile when Jamie approached. Jamie wanted to say something. *Thank you*, perhaps. Or *let's get coffee*. She only stared dumbly.

Vika said, "It was nice to meet you, Jamie."

Lumbering footfalls closed in, and both women turned.

Richard Barkley grinned stupidly at them. "Are you leaving without me?"

Vika replied, "I like to be unpredictable."

"You promised me a drink after this."

"Then you'd better collect your junk, because I am walking out this gate."

He backed up, beaming. "Give me two minutes."

Vika chuckled. "Okay."

The exchange left Jamie feeling awkward, and suddenly shy.

Vika touched her elbow. "Hey. You wanna get a coffee sometime?"

Jamie hugged her own middle. "Yeah. Yeah, I'd like that."

Vika took a pen and paper from her clutch, and jotted a quick note. "My number. Text, call, anytime. About anything." She held out the slip, and Jamie accepted it gratefully. Vika said, "And Jamie."

"Yeah."

"Listen, if you... if you ever find yourself backed into a corner and you don't know who to call, you call me. Okay?" Jamie received and returned an earnest stare.

Richard announced himself with all the subtlety of a marching band, after traversing the gardens with the pounding footfalls of a giant. "I'm ready."

Vika asked, "You have a car?"

"Brand new Falcon GTP, six speed manual with nineteen-inch alloys and—"

"Hey, Dick. As long as it has four wheels and functional doors, I'm good."

He beamed for Vika, but for Jamie was measured. "I'm sorry about Tannen. He can be a right ass sometimes." Jamie offered a weak smile.

Vika said, "Goodnight, Jamie."

"Good... goodnight. Both of you."

The two made their way out the gate, and as Jamie watched them cross the quiet street together, she was strangely relieved they weren't touching.

* * *

It was only the next day that Jamie sat outside a busy café, waiting for Vika to arrive. It was a gorgeous sunny afternoon, and a busker was belting out a tight rendition of *Baby it's You* with some talent, and yet more fervour.

Perhaps it'd been forward (and undeniably uncharacteristic) of Jamie to text Vika so soon after their meeting, but she felt completely comfortable in doing so, and she knew why. It was because Vika had meant what she'd said. Yes, at times people made offers out of politeness; offers they secretly hoped they would never be called upon to fulfill. But Jamie got not of whiff of insincerity from Vika. The offer of friendship was genuine, and Jamie's surety of it was only cemented when her text message received an almost instantaneous reply.

Jamie was scrolling through their conversation, when that serene voice finally called to her:

"Jamie Stevens." Vika was beaming, her eyes hidden behind sunglasses.

Jamie replied, "That's-a-mouthful-Malavika." Vika sat, and they exchanged smiles. Jamie said, "I hope it's okay that I messaged. It's such a beautiful day out, and, well... I really wanted to thank you for what you did last night."

"That's why I'm here? So you can thank me?"

God. Have I already cocked this up? "I don't know what you mean."

Vika lifted her shades and sat them on her crown. Then she studied Jamie with her dark but playful eyes. "Nothing to do with Richard?"

Jamie was doubly confused. "Wait, what, *Richard*? I... I don't know..."

"If I'd known there was something between the two of you—"

"Wait, stop. There is nothing between me and Richard. God, is that... is that what he told you?"

"Not in so many words." Vika tweaked a brow.

Jamie groaned. "Was he talking about me?"

"Maybe a little." Vika gave her a crooked smile, which Jamie found altogether disarming.

"We've known each other for ever. Not even a *close* forever, mind you. A distant forever."

"Jamie, have you been leading this guy on?"

"God, no!" Vika chuckled, and Jamie realised the woman was only teasing. Her hackles lowered, and a chuckle fell out of her as well. Jamie said, "I'm sorry if I ruined your date."

"It wasn't a date. I would never encroach upon your territory, Jamie."

"Oh my god, stop."

Vika's pleasure dimmed. "I'm not looking to date anyone right now. Things are... kinda crazy enough as it is."

Jamie saw the flicker of heartache in that quiet gaze. "You, ah... you wanna talk about it?"

For a moment, Jamie thought she might. But then that charming smile returned. "Not today. Tell me, what's the most humiliating thing Richard could tell me about you?"

Jamie propped her elbow on the table and rested her chin in her hand. "I don't think I want to answer that just yet. There might be no coffee number two."

Vika leaned over the table, close as though they'd been friends for years. "He's already told me some eye-popping things about you, Jamie Stevens. I'm still here."

"Oh, really? Like what?"

Vika slid back in her chair. "I think I'll keep you guessing for now."

"Oh, no. No, you don't, Vika. What is it? Did he tell you I pissed in one of his mum's potted plants? Because every time he tells that story, he forgets to mention I was five." Vika's mouth fell open. Then both women burst with laughter.

Then Vika's keen eye indicated she was thinking on a thing. Rather than rush, Jamie simply enjoyed the vision of her.

Vika finally said, "Richard was upset for you over the Tannen thing. I overheard him talking as though you were friends, so I introduced myself to him. I... I was curious about you. I hope that doesn't sound weird."

Jamie's first reaction to Vika's interest was abject shyness, and her cheeks burned. But something in the woman's subtle smile reassured her. "You don't have to talk to Richard. You can ask me anything."

The waitress finally delivered the order that Jamie had made, Vika's coffee of choice being a long black, and Jamie's an almond latte. Then they were alone again.

Vika said, "Listen, I should apologise to you for the party. I realise now the Bradbury's are good friends of yours. I didn't mean to put you in an awkward position."

"You didn't. Please don't apologise for that. I'm sorry I didn't say more in your defence."

"You said plenty. I was grateful."

"I wasn't exactly Louise to your Thelma."

Vika beamed. "Well, it's only early days yet." She lifted her mug. "Here's to a great year, Jamie."

Delighted, Jamie lifted her latte and chimed, "Here's to a great year, *Mal*."

Vika lowered her cup. "You *can't* call me *that*."

Jamie asked playfully, "Why not?!"

"For one thing, my surname is Lal. *Mal Lal* isn't exactly doing it for me. But mostly because *mal* is a prefix for all sorts of nastiness. Malformed, malpractice, malfeasance."

"Malfunction, maladjusted, malignancy."

"Ouch. Okay, I think the point has been sufficiently made."

Jamie chuckled. "How about *Mel*?"

Vika bunched a thoughtful brow. Then she lifted her long-black. "Here's to a great year, Jamie Stevens."

Jamie mirrored the gesture. "Here's to a great year, Mel Lal."

They bumped mugs, with Jamie already knowing they would be the best of friends.

It was so far distant that Mel couldn't have known what was coming for her. And she couldn't have known what it would mean - for her *or* for Jamie – when it finally did.

* * *

Blurb for Cicatrice:

2024 Firebird Book Award:
Category Award Winner Second: LGBTQ
Literary Titan:
Gold Book Award

What would you sacrifice for the person you love, for the one person who could never know how deeply you care? A gritty, action-packed thriller of family tragedy, insatiable vengeance and unwavering loyalty.

Jamie Stevens and Mel Lal were best friends at Melbourne University. More than that, they were family. But in October of 2008, something changed. Mel became anxious, secretive and distant. Then Jamie's life was turned upside down when Mel Lal disappeared.

Five years later, Mel resurfaces. She's been subjected to a nightmare that Jamie could not imagine, and Mel's only wish upon stumbling into Jamie again, is to protect the gentle writer from the hell that is Mel's existence: a relentless pursuit by a vindictive and sadistic arms dealer, hell bent on holding Mel accountable for a debt she can never repay.

Mel's feelings for Jamie have not faded with time, but Mel can never reveal the truth of them. To do so would put a target on Jamie's back. The chance reunion, however, sets in motion a series of events that spiral out of Mel's control, and it seems that after five years of running, the nightmare is only just beginning. If Mel can't stop Amir Hashim, all of her sacrifice to keep Jamie safe from a vicious, twisted madman... will have been for naught.

Testimonials

'A remarkable debut.' – *Literary Titan*

'Must-read sharp FF romance.' – *D. Silman, Reedsy Discovery*

'The book is a tour de force... an engaging read from beginning to end.' – *K. Lawley, Goodreads*

'The writing is nerve-wrackingly intense, and the scenes are engrossing. It is an unforgettable journey into the heart of darkness, but the light that shines through at the end is worth it.' – *Women Using Words*

'The story is so complex and woven like a tapestry...' – *Amber, Goodreads*

'This is an exceptionally well-written thriller...' – *Daja, Amazon*

'The plot kept me on the edge of my seat and the characters were so rich and beautifully written.' – *N. Zelniker, Goodreads*

EPILOGUE

May 1st
    11:03am

The taxi moved away, and its former occupant knocked on the door of a humble red-brick home, on a sedate urban street.

She stood back and smoothed her hair. Then she leaned her cane against the wall and brushed the sleeves of her white cotton shirt. She joined her hands in front and rocked on her feet.

When no one came, she turned to face the road. It was a fine autumn day, and the air smelled of freshly-mowed grass. The street was lined with maples shedding colourful leaves. Strollers meandered quietly by.

Despite the outer tranquillity, her insides were chaos.

Perhaps coming here was a mistake.

A catastrophic error had been made, and she couldn't know that it would be forgiven.

Soft noises came from inside.

She turned.

The door opened.

The woman who stood there was a shadow of the one who used to live here. Her eyes were heavy and darkly circled. She was thin; she was pale; her mascara was bleeding.

Upon recognition, her face performed a series of gestures. First, the brow bunched. Then it lifted. Then it scrunched. Then her mouth opened. Then it closed. The cheeks twitched. Her eyes squinted. Then her whole jaw quaked.

Say something to her, for goodness' sake.

"W..." But it got stuck. She cleared her throat. "Walnut."

Natalie puffed her cheeks, lips pressed so tight they almost disappeared. She shook her head: with denial, with distrust, with indictment. Not unwarranted.

"My... my beautiful Walnut. I am so sorry. I only just found out the letter was sent to you when it obviously shouldn't have been. I... I won't blame anyone else. It was my responsibility. It was a horrendous mistake and I am just so, so sorry."

Her eyes were so big; so weepy; so terribly vulnerable.

Everlee said, "I came as soon as I could. I'm okay, Walnut. They fixed my cauliflower brain. I'm still recovering, and I lost a little bit of my hair, but I'm doing well. Truly."

Natalie made no sound. She just stared, unblinking.

Everlee quietly begged, "Please, Walnut. Please, say something."

Natalie choked out a sob. Then she pulled Everlee inside of the snuggest embrace Everlee had ever received. Everlee flung arms tight around Natalie's waist, with no thought of letting go. Natalie's silence was broken by contagious crying, so that there were both blubbering wrecks at the threshold.

After many tears, Natalie let go so that she could gently stroke Everlee's cheeks. Her voice was frayed silk. "Since I read your letter, there is really only one thing I've wanted to say, one thing I so badly wished I'd said: I love you too, Ev."

There were many, many things for which Everlee Bertrand was thankful, but in that moment...

Oh, how she knew she was *truly* blessed.